Crown
&
Crumble

ALSO BY PIPER CJ

No Other Gods

The Deer and the Dragon

The Fox and the Falcon

The Night and Its Moon

The Night and Its Moon

The Sun and Its Shade

The Gloom Between Stars

The Dawn and Its Light

Accompanying *The Night and Its Moon* Novellas:

A Night Without Whispers

Wing and Arrow

A Year of Tea and Honey

Crown and Crumble

Villains

A Chill in the Flame

Fern's School for Wayward Fae

The Graveyard Gift

Crown & Crumble

moirai & daphne's story

PIPER CJ

To those of us tasked with breaking intergenerational curses—
It's a shitty, painful job, but it's worth it.

CONTENTS

LONG LIVE THE QUEEN

PART I
Pauper   3

PART II
Tiara   7

PART III
Crown   17

PART IV
Throne   29

PART V
Crown   35

UNTO US A PRINCESS IS BORN

PART I
Inheritance   43

PART II
Birthright   53

PART III
Reign   63

PART IV
Dynasty   67

Afterword   75
Content Warnings   77

The Deer and the Dragon   79

About the Author   93

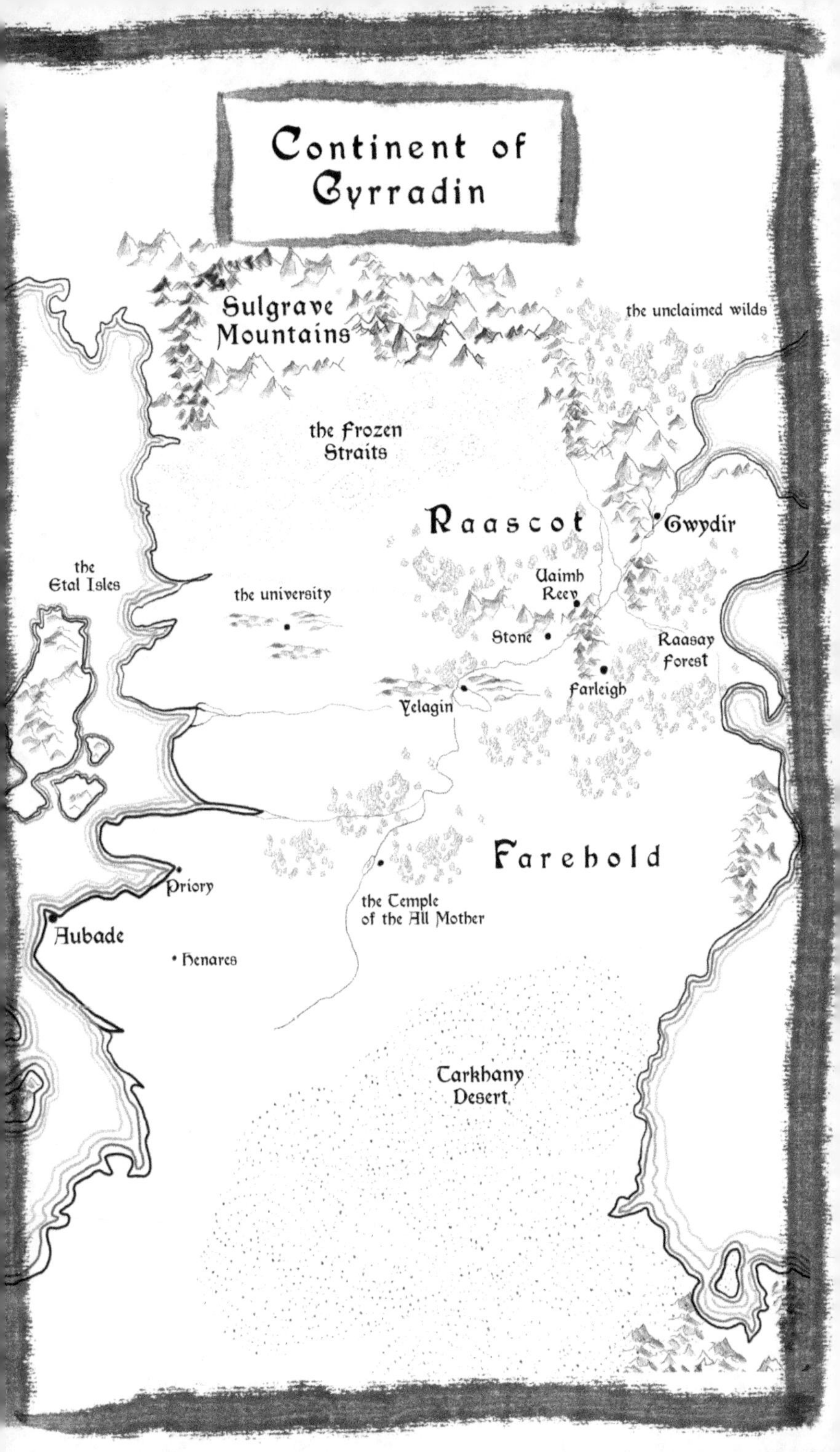

Continent of Cyrradin
Sulgrave Mountains
the unclaimed wilds
the Frozen Straits
Raascot
Gwydir
the Etal Isles
the university
Uaimh Reev
Stone
Raasay Forest
Farleigh
Yelagin
Farehold
Priory
the Temple of the All Mother
Aubade
Henares
Tarkhany Desert

LONG LIVE THE QUEEN
ACT I

PART ONE
PAUPER

Her heart pounded as her mother's face pinched in disappointment. She tried to swallow, but it was as if her mouth was filled with scratchy cotton. The woman began to remove her glove, and the little girl winced.

"Don't be a coward," her mother hissed. The burnt scent of brown sugar slithered along the cruel command. The girl hadn't been able to walk beside a pastry shop for years without her heart skipping anxiously as her mother's distinct perfume overpowered her. Nice things like cakes and pies filled her with dread, reminding her of little aside from anger and pain.

"Please," the girl begged, her word a single, pitiful request. She wanted to take a step backward, but knew better. The last time she'd attempted to escape a punishment, she'd learned how much crueler her mother could become.

Her mother's eyes narrowed into slits, then softened ever so slightly. She stared down at the child for a long moment before slowly putting her hand back into her glove. Cold afternoon light cut the space between them like the golden bars of a prison between the girl and her mother. Pieces of dust caught as the light moved. The sunny sparkles shone every bit as brightly as the diamond flecks of snow that drifted outside the cottage door.

"Father didn't care if I could use my gift or not," she whispered.

Her mother's next words dripped with poison. "Your father abandoned us for his ocean of whores. Let him go, and never think of him again. Fae men think they're gods, you foolish, stupid girl. He wasn't even full fae, yet he dared to treat me as if he was my superior? The half-breed isn't even my *equal*, yet out he stormed to take the world by the balls. The humans fall at their feet. Your father fancied himself too good for this shack, too good to raise a daughter, too good to be stuck in the rubbish by leaving you with me. Mark me, girl. We'll make him regret it. I'll have the last laugh when we show him who's truly too good. He was right."

She barely dared to repeat the word. "Right?"

"The humans. They should treat us as gods—even you, with your muddied blood, are so far above them. The world is ours to take. Ours."

"Please," the girl said again. Her heart cracked at the memory of him walking out the cabin door to leave her alone to starve, fed only melted snow, cruelty, and pain. He'd looked over his shoulder with his very human eyes—too small for his fae face—regret and pity flooding them as he regarded her helplessly. He'd never returned.

An unfamiliar sympathy crept into her mother's voice as she said, "Fae normally don't have to train this young. Pain is our rite of passage, but you will need to be far older than your years, girl. For that, I am sorry. But the royal family will be here by the end of the season, and if you don't have mastery over your gift, everything will fall apart. You need to be able to sustain it."

The girl's loose curls tickled her shoulders as she shook her head. "I can't. It's too hard."

"You can," her mother insisted. "You've held it for days at a time. By the time the first flowers bloom and the monarchs make their annual trip to see the tulip fields, you'll be ready. But you can't drop it. Not even for a minute. If you do…"

"We'll be found out."

"That's right," she agreed. The bars of golden light flexed and curved as she stepped through them, kneeling in front of her daughter. "And if we're found out?"

"We'll be killed."

"We'll be killed," her mother agreed.

The girl's lip began to quiver, and she was quite certain that she would cry. Her mother's eyes hardened. The harder she fought the urge, the more intense the choking need to release her tears became. "But why? Why can't we stay here? Why can't we—"

Her ears popped against the pain as a high-pitched ringing filled the cabin. Her eyes widened, but she knew better than to cry out. She felt blood rush to the place on her cheek where her mother had struck her.

Her mother looked at her as if she was a spoiled bite of meat pie that needed to be spat into a napkin. "Do you know how many people get to be queens and princesses?"

Tears streamed silently down the girl's face. She straightened her shoulders, standing as tall as she could as she said: "Two."

Her mother nodded.; "That's right. Only two. We are not destined for a shack. We are so much better than your father. Two women get to be the most powerful beings in Gyrradin. Right now, it's Queen Penelope and Princess Moirai. We won't have long to act, but I have a plan. I'll wear the face of the farmer's wife and bid them in to collect their bouquets—just for the women. First, I'll take care of the princess—don't make that ungrateful face. Not now, not ever again." Her mother stopped short to snarl. She steadied her breathing before she said, "Once I've killed the queen, I can wear her face. It may take a moment to step into her things, so we'll have to act quickly. Now, repeat it back to me. Once you master your gift, we can never use your name again. Once you master your gift, you must hold it forever, before men and fae alike. The world will be yours to take. There's only one name you can answer to it. Tell me what it is."

"Moirai."

PART TWO
TIARA

King Aden made a sour face. "Since when does she not like lemon tarts?"

Queen Penelope smiled dreamily and patted her husband's hand. "She loves them, dear. She's just going through a phase. You'll clean your plate, won't you, sweetie?"

The changeling now known as Princess Moirai anticipated the pinch before she felt it. Her mother bit into the tender skin of her thigh with her thumb and forefinger. Moirai's nostrils flared against the pain, but it was the only action she permitted herself. Nausea roiled through her. She hated lemon. It was only put on rancid food in their village to help mask the taste of rotting meat. Every lemon-soaked bite had required a watchful eye, lest she bite into a wriggling maggot.

Her mother had assured her that the acid from the lemon helped to make the food clean and edible, but several nights retching over the bin until her back muscles spasmed made her doubt the veracity of those claims. Still, they'd had neither money nor options. She could eat, or she could starve. Now, she'd rather die than eat anything flavored with lemons.

Moirai picked up the tart and plastered a false, wide smile on her face. She didn't miss the charred layer of burnt brown sugar that glazed the top. Two of the worst things on the goddess's lighted earth, and she needed to face them with courtly decorum. "Thank you, Father," she said to the king. He watched her disapprovingly as she bit into the tart, eyeing her as she chewed and swallowed. Then King Aden grunted and returned to his meal.

Sweat prickled her forehead. The room began to spin ever so slightly. She was going to be sick, and if she was sick, she wasn't sure if she could maintain her illusion.

Though they'd been in castle for nearly nine months. Nine months of wishing for a return to their country cabin, of mourning the face she'd never wear again, of struggling to keep her chin high in her gilded jail. She still lost the outer edges of her gift when she wasn't careful. Her sudden loss of the ability to play the harp after years of training had baffled and frustrated her teachers to no end. She'd done her best to practice late into the night, but her mother had walked in on her sobbing with frustration, fingers swollen, canines glistening in the castle's torchlight as her full fae features were on display for all to see. Of course, her mother's solution was always the same. She fixed things through violence. If Moirai could learn to maintain the illusion even under the most dire of situations, then she'd never be caught unaware and make a mistake in front of the court.

Unlike Penelope, Moirai was not a true shapeshifter. As such, Moirai had not been able to hold any illusions while asleep. This wouldn't have been a problem, had Moirai not had a blessing scheduled for morning's first light. The handmaiden who'd discovered the pointed ears of a fae girl in the princess's bed had screamed.

The attendant had lived roughly one minute longer from the time the scream had left her mouth to the time Queen Penelope had jammed a pair of shears meant for trimming hair into her throat.

"Cast the illusion!" Penelope had whispered. The hour was early enough that Moirai could barely make out the grey, shocked horror on her mother's face. The first purples of dawn had filtered in through the curtains that had been pulled back by now-dead hands, a poor woman who'd seen something she was never meant to see.

Moirai had fumbled with her sheets, struggling through her shock to see the lifeless body and the blood dripping from the knife.

"Moirai, do it now!" Penelope's voice had been caught between command and plea as the sounds of footsteps, no doubt in answer to the scream, had sounded from down the hall.

Moirai could hardly breathe. There was a dead body. Someone had seen her fae form, her gem-colored eyes, her sharpened teeth, her angelic skin, and sounded a primal alarm. "But, what will you—"

"She tried to kill you." Penelope had tightened her grip around the scissors. The motion had caused a few more droplets to shake loose from the end of the shears, creating a ripple from the crimson puddle slowly forming around the lifeless maid.

The footsteps grew louder.

"Now, Moirai!"

And she had. By the time armed men had burst into the room, they had seen two royal women, and the slain servant who'd be buried in disgrace as someone who'd attempted to assassinate the princess.

From then on, guards were stationed outside of Princess Moirai's door that so that no one would go in and out, morning or night, without the queen's permission. Locks were installed that could be unlocked from only the inside. The royal guard had protested against the wisdom of this choice, but the queen's maternal paranoia won out, and the court was forced to oblige. The queen, breaking tradition, had demanded that their rooms adjoin. It had left Moirai in a state of constant threat, knowing morning or night, she was never safe from her mother's lessons.

Behind the prison of locked doors, no one would burst in on Moirai. And no one would save her from the lessons her mother bestowed. The first of which included two bottles of healing tonic, a crimson syrup for pain, and the very shears that had ended the life of her attendant slicing into the arched flesh of her fae ears. Horrid scars would be the only thing that remained under the curled locks she wore long and loose, regardless of the fashion of the day. It was better to be mutilated than to be fae.

It was both blessing and curse that her gift for illusion allowed her to cover split lips, swollen eyes, and black-and-blue bruises. The cuts were not given the aid of healing tonic. The split cracked brows and damaged tissue scarred and sagged, her youthful face tilting and moving as if she were a teenager covered in wrinkles. If she'd had no gift for illusion, they might have thought her an ugly hag rather than the tortured young woman she was. Her lines marked not years as they did with humans and the passage of time, but fights, impolite words, annoying coughs, and disappointments. Unfortunately, her gift could do nothing about accompanying limps or speech impediments, so her mother had to find creative ways to perpetuate her abuse.

The spinning hall tore her from her memories. Moirai planted her feet on the stones beneath her and focused on her breathing. She fixed her eyes on something on the far end of the hall and watched it with steadying clarity. She listened to the clinking of forks and knives, the swallowing and chewing of those around her, and inhaled deep breaths of roast chicken and salt pork that lingered through the banquet hall.

It was fortunate that King Aden and Queen Penelope had

not been known for any particularly loving relationship. They'd been an arranged marriage and bore a child out of obligation. It seemed from some whispers that Penelope would be expected to try again for a second heir, should her only child be barren, but Moirai couldn't allow that to be her problem. Aden was attentive neither as husband, nor father, which was fortunate. The man had scarcely known the daughter of his own flesh and blood. He wouldn't notice the very things that might give them away as changelings. She wasn't sure what was common in monarchies, but discovered both relief and blessing upon learning the king would only see Moirai only on formal occasions when tradition demanded the entire royal family's presence.

This was such a time.

When I'm queen, Moirai thought to herself, *I'll have every lemon tree banished from the kingdom. No one will be able to disobey me.*

Her stomach turned once more, but it was not the residual flavor of tart that bothered her. Her mother was fae. As such, the woman may never perish. Lemon trees would be allowed to thrive. Beatings would continue. And Moirai would never be queen.

"You have a new tutor," came a voice from behind her as Queen Penelope burst into the rooms without knocking. Green flashed in the corner of her eye as she spun. She thought her mother's emerald gown made her look more snake-like than usual.

Moirai remained seated at the vanity, frozen in the midst of dousing herself in a cocktail of perfumes provided by her servants. Unlike her mother, whose baked-good smell could conceivably be manufactured, Moirai's was too unique a fae mark to leave unattended. She once knew her scent to be loose-leaf green tea and freshly turned earth. She couldn't chance such a delicate continuity on the noses of her people and risk suspicion, so instead she bathed in musky, matronly sprays.

Now sixteen, she'd spent the last eight years mastering court politics, learning how to maintain her illusion under all circumstances, and how to appease the mother she'd grown to hate with every fiber of her being. She cursed herself for not listening more carefully for footsteps. Her hand flew to her chest to force her heart from beating out of its cage as adrenaline pumped through her. Behind Queen Penelope trailed a tall, beautiful man with the amber hair of the south, and the bronze skin of the north. His tailored shirt clung tight to his chest. A cloud of aged scotch and suede wafted in on an unseen wind. The verdant wreaths of his eyes were too big, too...

He was fae. Perhaps not fully fae from the looks of it, much like Moirai in her truest form. His features suggested his heritage was one of mingled kingdoms.

Moirai's eyes widened.

"Don't worry," Queen Penelope said coolly, "your gift is safe with us. Your father needn't know. This is Cassius. He's quite the powerful healer, and a member of our royal guard. He's been responsible for the fae in your father's army and has a history of tutelage within the small magics. He is sworn to secrecy, as am I. We are the only two in the kingdom who know you're in possession of a small magic. Such abilities are rare in humans, but..."

Penelope's eyes chilled as her stare bored into Moirai's soul, daring her to speak.

Moirai shook her head slowly. "I don't need a tutor."

"I'd like to see if you can replicate your small magic," Penelope said. "Try to cast an illusion to make your bedside candle disappear, as you did for me. Cassius has trained the fae in your father's guard and helped them to unlock their abilities. While you're human, a fae would be best in helping you master the ultimate expansion of your small magic. Cassius is quite adept at such things."

The wordless exchange was both desperation and challenge.

"Do it again," Penelope clipped.

Moirai was aghast. She'd held her illusion under literal torture. She wouldn't break it under pain, under panic, under any shock or horror the world had in store. Her mother had been the greatest trainer and most abhorrent nightmare, born of hell itself. How could the woman possibly expect her to do anything more?

"Make the candle disappear." The Queen's lip twitched as she waited. Moirai didn't know what cruel trick her mother was playing, though the woman never did anything unless it directly served her.

"If I may," Cassius cut in. The look on Penelope's face was as if a rodent had scurried across her foot. No one in the court dared speak over her. Moirai held her breath as she watched the tutor. His voice was so much deeper than Moirai had expected. There was a low, soothing molasses to the sound, soothing and delicious all at once. "I train alone, Your Majesty."

Penelope flexed the fingers dangling at her sides before wrapping them into tight fists. "My daughter—"

"You are the Queen Mother, and I am the trainer. With respect, Your Majesty, please leave us be. I swear to you, if Princess Moirai is truly predisposed to the small magics, she will leave my tutelage having mastered the furthest reaches of her abilities."

The knot in Moirai's throat bobbed as she looked between her mother and Cassius. After a frigid eternity, Penelope nodded once. She said nothing as she exited the room. The moment the door latched, Moirai jumped up from her stool and ran to the door to lock it behind them. Relief trickled down her spine knowing that, at least for the moment, she was safe.

She leaned her forehead against the cool wood, savoring the delicious barricade. Freedom was so rare, she'd nearly forgotten the tutor before he spoke again.

"She's an intense woman, the Queen."

Moirai scrunched her eyes into tightly controlled emotion before she turned to face him. "That she is."

"And," he said carefully, "knowing that magic is typically unlocked through trauma, I might be so bold as to venture a guess as to how your gift was discovered."

She didn't blink as she stared at him.

"Are you safe?"

Moirai nearly choked on her laugh. She sank to the floor, back still against the door, in a very un-princess-like moment of surrender. The skirts of her dress pooled on the floor as a single bitter tear accompanied her acidic humor.

He remained quiet for a while. "And the candle? How is it that she knows your gift was illusion, rather than transmutation? Perhaps you sent it away, then called it back?"

Moirai fought the urge to touch the disfigured remnants of her ears. She hardly remembered what she'd looked like. Due to her father's mixed blood, she hadn't inherited the too-large eyes, but the breathtaking tourmaline gradient of her irises—a celestial emerald fading into magenta just around her pupils—were of unmistakably fae coloration. The deadly points of her fangs, the ethereal glow of her skin. She'd been able to run her fingers along her teeth, her ears, even while wearing the stolen princess's plain, human face. She supposed it belonged to only her, now. She'd been the only princess the continent had known for many, many years.

"We could feel the candle," Moirai said quietly. "It was still there."

"But your mother seems to believe you have the gift of illusion, rather than invisibility. There's been another instance, then? In addition to making a candle disappear, have you also perhaps created something new? Something that wasn't there before?"

Defeat smothered her. She was a husk as the man spoke to her. Why had her mother sent this trainer to her room? What more could she possibly want? Moirai had given everything she had to give. Now she had to lie and defend her abuser to cover their crimes. No one could know of the murder and treason that had bloodied their paths to royalty.

"Yes," was all she said.

He exhaled through his nose. Shoving his hands into his pockets, he took a few casual steps toward her. "Humans are often terrified of magic. I don't fault you for your exhaustion, or your mother for her caution. I will safeguard your secrets. But your power is nothing to fear, and certainly nothing that should bring you shame. You're next in line to be queen, Princess Moirai. Who knows what sort of secret treasure this gift may have uncovered?"

PART THREE
CROWN

"I should go." Cassius rolled onto his side, bronze hair unbound and tumbling over his shoulders as he leaned to kiss her. She met his lips, savoring the taste of scotch. The silken sheet tugged slightly at the motion, revealing the broad expanse of his chest, the width of his shoulders, the strong arms she'd come to know and love so deeply. He looked at home amidst the fleur-de-lis and finery. His heavenly face was art finer than anything that hung on the walls of her elaborately decorated chambers.

"I have a better idea," Moirai said, pushing the sweat-damp curls out of her eyes.

He flashed the brilliant, charming smile that had opened the door to both her heart and her bed. "Tell me, Oh Wise One."

"Do you remember my nineteenth birthday? The banquet—"

His grin widened. "With the Viscount! Goddess almighty, Moirai, your gift is useful, but I was certain we'd be caught. The man sat directly in my lap!"

"Oh my goddess, that banquet would have been unbearable without you! I could barely breathe in that horrid dress. And the way they paint my face whenever I go to events…"

He mock-grimaced. "Are the attendants also to blame for why you wear a perfume better suited for a grandmother than a flower of twenty-two?" Cassius leaned into her, nuzzling into her hair as he said, "Your natural scent is so much lovelier, Rai. I wish you would just be yourself."

Joy was an emotion she only felt in his presence. He liked her mind, her wit, her words. He believed in her gifts, and empowered her at every turn. Her airy laugh was one of pure pleasure as she recalled the memory. "Come with me to the party, Cass. No one needs to know you're there. We've learned our lesson! We'll keep you standing rather than have people perceive an empty chair. You don't have to leave."

"You can't ask the commoner who warms your bed for such things."

Her lower lip lifted. "You can't possibly believe that's all you are to me."

His face softened, and she knew exactly what he was about to say. His expression poked a small hole within her, draining the happy light that had filled her only moments before.

"It's not just that, Rai. You know I have—"

She'd heard it before and couldn't take another word. "I'm to be queen."

He huffed, extending a hand in a failed attempt to pull her close.

Moirai sat up in bed. She clutched the sheet against her defensively. She'd been naked before him one thousand times, but this fight laid her far barer than mere flesh. She fought the urge to tear the thick tapestry from the bronze rods and clothe herself with something too dense for harsh realities to penetrate the tightly woven fabrics. "How can you still choose her?"

Cassius reached for the hand balled against the sheet, but she yanked it away. She turned her back on him and stormed from the bed, forcing him to see her in an opaque shift. He wasn't worthy of her shape, her skin, the loveliness of the young, unmarked human princess. Not now. Not with another woman's name on his tongue.

"My betrothal to Amina was arranged years before I met you. And you were a child—"

"I was sixteen!" she glared, spinning on him. "I was old enough to know what I wanted. I was old enough to have eyes only for you, years before you looked at me with those same eyes that gaze into mine when I'm in your arms, when you're within me. I saved myself for you, Cassius. I've been with no one else."

He pulled on his pants but remained shirtless as he stepped toward her. "And I've never asked that of you."

"Ask it now!"

His chest expanded with a slow, patient breath. "You're to be queen, yes. You cannot be with your trainer. You cannot ask me to take no wife, no lover, no—"

"I'm to be Farehold's ruler, and if I choose someone of common blood, the choice is mine to make! But you needn't be of common blood, Cassius. Don't you see? I can make the people see a man of royal lineage. You know I can! I can turn you into a Duke, into a Marquis, into a—"

"Stop."

She hated herself for the tears that carved hot, salty lines down her face. They pooled in the space below her chin and streamed down her neck, wetting the same bare breasts he could no longer see while she held the illusion of her shift. "You don't love her, Cass. You haven't seen this estranged fiancée of yours in, what, ten years? If she won't forsake Raascot for you, then how can she truly love you?!"

"She's fae, Rai. I may not match her blood, but I'll live for centuries. Amina may very well live forever, should the goddess wish it. Raascot is my home, too."

"It isn't! Your father is both human and from Farehold. You

have gifts of the light fae. You were conscripted by Aubade. You belong here."

"You're fully human, Rai. I don't expect you to understand how hard it is for fae in the south. My parents have built a full life in the north. They've put down roots for me by securing a good match. We all know how lucky I was to find a suitor as a halfling, which may not be something you appreciate, but I do. They're good people who've paved a path for me once I'm released from conscription. It's where I'll return."

She knew exactly how difficult life was for southern fae, though she couldn't tell him that. She hated being conde-scended to about wielding one's abilities, even though she was three-quarters fae and possessed even more blood and magic than he. She detested the fae pieces of herself, the ones in him, and cursed Amina with her untainted, full-fae blood. She wiped at her cheeks, loathing how pathetic she must look.

His brows met. She detested the sorrow and regret painting itself across his face. "The heart knows little of obligations. Isn't that what brought us here, to your sheets? But Amina and I are similarly duty-bound. She can no more leave her post than I mine. I'll return to Raascot when I'm released from the crown's service. For all I know, you'll have left the earth and gone to be with the All Mother long before I cross the northern border, Rai. For now, my oaths keep me here. But I will not break my vow to her."

He stretched out a large hand to cup her chin, but she turned away. She bore holes into the ground with her hateful gaze. "You broke your vow to Amina the moment you took me to bed. You've broken your vow to her every day for years."

Ignoring her denial of his affection, he cupped her cheek and forced her to look him in the face. "Spare me, Princess. You're trying to sneak your lover into your fucking engage-ment party this very night. In one month's time you'll walk down the aisle in white, surrounded by courtiers, and say your vows before the goddess. You understand your duty, and you will fulfill it. You will reign side by side when your fiancé becomes the prince of the land, and one day the two of you will ascend the throne. And you do not need a low-born trainer complicating your life simply because you're in possession of one of the small magics."

Her lip quivered as she looked helplessly at him. "There's nothing small about my magic, Cass. This isn't a party trick where I can light a wick with a spark of flame. I can turn you into *him*. I can give you his face. You know I can."

This was precisely why Penelope had forced her to stretch her gifts in the first place. The queen secured her deceit, knowing she could force her daughter to conjure necessary figureheads while disappearing others. Penelope's arrogance kept her from worrying that Moirai would ever use this gift of her own volition. At times like this, Moirai wondered if her mother was right to think her spineless.

"Don't say things like that."

Moirai glared. "Then I'll never release you from your service. You'll be forced to stay in Farehold! You'll—"

He tightened his hold on her chin. "Don't be cruel. You'll have the world at your fingertips, and you'll be able to use that brain and wit to bend the continent to your will. You are many things, but you are not your mother."

She slapped his hand away and grabbed for her true shift. Perhaps it wouldn't make a difference for him, but she no longer felt comfortable in her own skin. "Maybe I should become her," she said bitterly.

His nostrils flared, fists balling at the horrible implications of her threat.

"Do it," he challenged. "Keep me indebted to you. The human life is short, Princess. Bind me to you until your dying day."

"You know nothing, Cassius. I—" She bit her words off before making the foolish error of proclamation. She could live every bit as long as he. She could spend one thousand years as queen, never letting him leave her employ. Perhaps she'd say she'd been blessed by the All Mother for long life. Maybe she'd claim she'd discovered the fountain of youth, or was in possession of the resurrection stone, never aging, never changing. She was Moirai, the unexplainable rebirth of the goddess, Farehold's princess forevermore.

He stared intently for the broken thought to conclude, but she let it hang between them.

"Go," she said bitterly.

He looked into her eyes with love, and sadness, and compassion. Cassius gathered his things and pulled his shirt over his head, his posture and expression reflecting every bit of agony she felt.

"Rai—"

"I don't want to hear it."

He straightened his shoulders, crestfallen as he looked at her. "I do love you."

She blinked through tears. "I don't believe you."

"You don't have to believe it. It's—"

Years of abuse had taught her to listen for footsteps. She could hear a needle clatter to the floor a room away, always on edge for her mother's arrival. She knew shifts in mood, could read body language, anticipated what would or wouldn't set her off. But her greatest ally had become her nose. In the split second it took for her to inhale the scent of brown sugar, she threw her hand up in response. Her door banged open on its hinges as Queen Penelope stormed into the room in a flourish of crinkling gold fabric. The ostentatious crown atop her head glinted in the light. Moirai kept her hand angled, index finger pointed in a stilling signal as she cast her illusion over Cassius. He froze, not breathing, not so much as blinking as her mother marched toward the center of the room.

Moirai wasn't offered the chance to so much as open her mouth to ask why the queen was here before a high, loud slap took her breath away. She gasped against the pain, but she did not cower or wince or cry. She set her teeth and narrowed her eyes.

"You *whore*," dripped Penelope's venomous insult. "Tell me why the servants were gossiping about the moans from the bedchambers of a *betrothed* princess. Tell me why their whispers are of your ruined virtue, Moirai."

Any pain she'd felt moments prior was set ablaze as hatred consumed her. Her lips pulled back in an answering snarl as she rose to meet the storm. "I don't know what occupies the servants, mother. I have better things to do than sully myself by eavesdropping on commoners."

Penelope barked a laugh. "After everything I've done for you, you would see it in ruins. We're meant to show your father who will have the last laugh for what he did to us, and you would burn it to the ground. You would destroy our *kingdom* because you lend your body to—"

She bristled at her father's memory. The final moments of his hesitation on the threshold would be forever burned into her mind. She didn't blame him for wanting a life away from his horrid wife, but she despised any man who would abandon a child to suffer such cruelties. He was meant to be her protector, and he'd failed her. He'd failed them both. Maybe her mother was right, though she loathed the thought of the woman being correct, even for a moment. Fae men were brought into the world to do little more than disappoint.

"Spare me, mother. I'll try to fuck more quietly. Or perhaps I'll scream. If they're going to talk, I may as well put on a show."

"Tell me who. *Who* do I have to thank for my ungrateful curse of a child who has been handed a literal kingdom, a child I've elevated from rags to crowns, only for her to shred it with her naked body?"

Moirai's eyes were scarcely more than slits as she said, "The stable boy, the cook, the bishop, the—"

Penelope raised her hand, but Moirai remained stone-still,

her unflinching glare a challenge. The queen lowered it slowly, choosing to strike with words instead. "Word will get back to the king, if it hasn't already. Do you know what that means?"

Moirai made a show of nonchalance. "That the engagement is off? Oh, shit. Tell the sop for me, will you?"

"No, you disappointing cow. It means I'm going to have to take care of Farehold's king because *you* couldn't keep your animal urges at bay. You're no better than a human."

The temperature in the room seemed to shift as Moirai listened.

"Humans have never betrayed me, mother. Maybe it was the human pieces of father that almost made him stay. It's the goddess-damned fae—" She halted in the midst of her tirade, absorbing her mother's message. "When you say *take care* of…"

Penelope had grown colder with age. She'd never been one for compassion, but ice frosted each word as she spat, "What? It's regicide? It's treason? Two royals are fine, but by the third, you develop a backbone? I'd see the blood drain from a thousand monarchs before I let you take this from me. We weren't handed a kingdom, Moirai. I built it brick by brick through blood and pain. I will defend what I've created."

The tender muscle beneath Moirai's eye twitched slightly as she fought the urge to look at Cassius. She saw him in her periphery, statuesque as he stared on as an expressionless sentinel to their darkest sins.

"Mother," Moirai dropped her voice to a scarcely audible threat. "If the servants hear rumors of my infidelity, then surely the walls have ears. I'd be very careful as to what you say next."

Penelope's lips pulled into a tight line. It was anger, admonishment, and concession at once. She was right, and her mother knew it. Some secrets were never to be spoken of, but it was not the walls who bore witness. Penelope had already shouted their bloodiest skeletons in a fit of rage. How many would die tonight to contain the soulless woman's misstep?

"Tonight is your banquet." Penelope's whisper matched her daughter's, the low, frosted tone. "Can you pull yourself together to meet the man who is to be your husband? Aden will maintain appearances whether or not he's heard the rumors. It may be your last night experiencing the king's mercy. And if your fiancé hears…"

"Conspire with someone else," Moirai said flatly. "There is nothing more I can do for your schemes. I wash my hands of this."

Penelope wrinkled her nose. "Wash your hands of me, and scrub the shame and cum from your body. You smell of sex and…" Her mother paused. Her face changed as she inhaled through her nose once more.

Moirai's lips parted slightly. From across the room, she saw Cassius's eyes widened.

"…Scotch," Penelope concluded. "It's him, isn't it."

Ice pumped through her veins. "Who?"

"Don't lie to me."

Moirai shook her head. "I don't know what you're talking about."

A single terse laugh. "Denial betrays you. The best lies are born of truths, girl. Or, after all we've been through, have I failed to teach you deceit? Cassius. I've smelled spirits on you before, but I would have much preferred believing my daughter has given herself over to drink than to think you've set your maidenhood ablaze and risked what we've fought to earn for the hired help."

Moirai clapped her hands slowly. "Are you proud of the sleuth you've become? He visits me daily. Does it bring you peace to know a fae male left with mussed hair and a satisfied smile? Congratulate yourself. You're the one who brought my lover into my life."

Time had killed the frightened child within her. All that remained was the monster desiring to bite back. She poked the proverbial bear, and she waited.

"Guards!" Penelope's voice echoed through the room. She turned on her heel and threw open the door, shouting for them again. Moirai watched in petrified horror. Was the woman so mad she'd have her own daughter arrested? Had she somehow guessed Cassius was still in the room? Moirai looked to Cassius, but could say nothing of what she felt. She couldn't apologize. She couldn't explain. She couldn't beg for forgiveness, or plead with him not to tell others of what he'd learned. She wasn't sure whether she should be terrified for him or of him, but however this night ended, she would know no peace.

"Your Majesty!" The guard snapped to attention before her. Clanging metal echoed off the cream stones of Castle Aubade as others rushed to join their comrade. Penelope's tyrannical reputation had seeped far beyond the domestic walls of her daughter's room. The staff and civilians trembled whenever she called. This was no exception.

"Send an armed guard to the home of one Cassius of Raascot. My daughter's former tutor is to be brought up on charges of attempted rape. And when I discover who was on watch and left Princess Moirai susceptible to violence and did nothing to intervene, they will be hanged within the hour."

The guard swallowed audibly.

"What are you waiting for?" She pointed an accusatory finger. "Go!"

"Yes, Your Grace." The collection of guards turned to do her bidding.

The bones in Moirai's legs became little more than pudding as she trembled. She watched in horror as the queen rested her fingers on the doorframe. Penelope threw a single, satisfied look over her shoulder before disappearing into the hallway and closing the door behind her.

Moirai and Cassius stayed suspended in time as the seconds ticked into minutes. The sun inched its way across the sky above the ocean. Seabirds called out. Life went on. But still, Cassius did not move.

Moirai was the first to let her head drop. She buried her face in her hands and sank to the floor. Her sobs were noiseless as her body shook. Her mother had taken her childhood, her agency, her identity, her desires, her love, and smashed them underfoot, driving them into the dirt like the very caramel buns Moirai could never again consume, gagging on the traumatic scent of brown sugar.

A hand rested on her shoulder, but she didn't look up.

"You are not Princess Moirai," came Cassius's quiet voice.

Still, her face remained covered by her hands while she cried.

"Have I ever met her? The true-born princess?"

What could she say? There was no lie that would serve her. He'd heard it all from her mother's mouth. Moirai shook her head slowly through her sobs. No. He hadn't. No one had in many, many years, but that seemed unimportant now.

"Penelope—she is truly your mother?"

Moirai didn't understand his interrogation, but looked up through swollen eyes, knowing her face must match. She pulled in choppy, ragged breaths as she nodded. There was nothing she could say. There were no lies she could spin.

"Look at me, Rai."

Moirai obliged, though it filled her with dread. She expected him to look at her with disgust, but she could scarcely discern the emotions behind his eyes. "Wash your face. Get dressed. Go to your engagement banquet. I will meet you tonight. Do you understand?"

She hiccupped through the labored breathing of her thick sorrow. It took several rapid blinks to clear the tears from her vision. "But—"

"Tonight. After the banquet."

PART FOUR
THRONE

Penelope liked three things.

She enjoyed the appreciative whispers of her ageless beauty, glad to have stolen a face that, even for a human, was rather lovely. The years went on, but Farehold's queen seemed to have halted in time, forever trapped in the late monarch's last moment before she'd slit the woman's throat behind the tulip fields.

She liked the royal closets, filled with rooms and rooms of gowns, jewels, capes, diamond-encrusted heels, bangles, furs, and riches.

Most of all, she liked that she'd become the closest thing the continent would ever know to the whispered fables of a manifester. She'd wished herself queen, and queen she'd become. She snapped her fingers and asked for fruit pies and honeyed ham and a painting of her favorite horse, and they were made. She commanded a life be taken, and it was snuffed out. She created buildings, vaults, marriage arrangements, negotiations, fear, and life, all from the sheer force of want. She wasn't entirely convinced that she wasn't the All Mother herself.

Penelope hated three things.

She detested the audacity it took for King Aden to dare approach her chambers. A disgusting human, barely more than a primal animal, had no business breathing her air, let alone touching her.

She hated the whispers of the servants regarding her daughter. They'd heard nothing of sex or love. Instead, other words had carried among the laundresses and through the maidens. The daffodils in the castle gardens were vibrantly fertilized with the decomposing body of the servant Penelope had killed so she might wear her face from time to time, should she need to don plain clothes and partake in gossip. It was the best way to ensure that no one had ever caught wind of their changeling queen and princess. What she'd learned from their hushed tones had made her stomach turn.

Princess Moirai had not bled in one month's time.

She'd failed to get her daughter to despise men, a failure that was perhaps her one fault. Penelope should have focused her educationed on important matters of the sexes. Penelope was allowed a flaw, she supposed, so she forgave herself the oversight. Everyone made mistakes. If she acted quickly, this might be an error she could fix with a rushed wedding.

Most of all, she hated that there was no audience to appreciate her genius.

It seemed terribly unfair that her filthy half-blood of a former husband didn't know she currently reigned as the single most important person in the world. Perhaps she could have him seized and brought before her. She was more or less the goddess, after all.

It would have been nice to have an adoring fan to explain how she'd stolen their crowns, maintained their cover, and taken every step to secure her future. She puckered her lip in a pout as she looked down at the lifeless body of her daughter's former trainer.

Of course she'd known Cassius was in the room.

Unlike her ruined daughter and the mixed lover, she had a perfect fae nose. She knew the difference between a lingering scent and one rolling off a presence. Sending guards to seize him would ensure two things. The first was that he would not go home. The second was that he would rest safely, sloppily, confident that they'd tricked her into thinking he was not hidden in Moirai's bedroom, so she'd know exactly where to find him.

Idiot.

Not all powers were quite so violent as hers, but had her young sister not mysteriously and without any provocation whatsoever lost her footing as a child, she wouldn't have known that death was what it took for her to take a face. In Penelope's defense, it had been her turn to play with the doll. Her sister shouldn't have been greedy.

Penelope had felt immense fear at being caught, panic at what she'd do with the broken body, thrill at the rush of power, and the overwhelming flood of emotions had unlocked something within her. When she'd dipped her hands in the wash basin to clean them of blood, she'd looked into eyes that belonged not to her, but to her prim, perfect sister.

A sister that, if Penelope was right, her parents may never have to know was dead.

It may have been a challenging ruse to maintain, as surely they'd want both of their children in bed as they bestowed bedtime kisses and blew out the candles, but wearing a false face would buy her the time she needed to hatch a plan.

Death was such a clean solution.

When she took a life and stepped into its shoes, there was no one to tell her tales, no one to raise warning bells, no one to ask questions, as she could simply craft a new narrative while wearing the face of the life she'd taken. She had been worried, of course, when she'd taken on her father's features, that she wouldn't be able to step into her sister's skin again. Her anxiety had been short-lived, as each skin remained as a trophy of her kills. She would have hated remaining a man, and probably wouldn't have passed for her father for very long, as she could mimic his features, but not his fae gifts. He couldn't have gone on living, though. Not after he'd confided in her deceased sister that he suspected his firstborn was insane. He had planned to smuggle her sister and mother out of the house and leave her behind? That was true insanity.

Her gift was imperfect.

Though she'd coveted the kind, handsome faeling who'd sold her family fruits at so many markets, he'd had eyes for none but his wife. The woman had screamed like a stuck pig when killed. Unfortunately, ~~but~~ his late wife's death had not been as satisfying as she'd hoped.

She had crawled into his bed that night to kiss him, to be held by him, to make love to him at long last, but had seen the questions flicker in his eyes as the candle's wick smoked out. The harder she had tried to become his lost wife, the less he had cared for her.

So much for his vows.

He'd promised to love her forever, and yet here he was, breaking his word simply because she didn't share exact personality traits of the woman who'd once worn this skin. What a fickle, horrible man. She'd been wrong to love him—stupid, even—but he'd filled her belly with a daughter. Her pregnancy had been a useful enough bargaining chip when he'd packed to leave, buying her four more years in his company.

The girl's gift was not as bloody as her own, but every bit as useful.

Perhaps the man had been an utter disappointment, but the child had provided her with a unique opportunity. Together, they had accomplished an infiltration that she alone would not have managed.

But her tool, her curly-haired wrench against the cogs of ambition, her muddy human-fae crossbreed, had dared to thwart her plans. Fortunately for Penelope, she was three steps ahead at all times. The borrowed face of a servant had rushed into Moirai's bedroom, claiming the princess had sent her. She'd hurried the escaping Cassius into a secret passage.

He hadn't died after the first blow to the head, but his shock had bought her the time to strike again, and again.

Moments later, Penelope shifted into the long-disused form of her father as she grunted and tugged and pulled the trainer's body from the tunnels to the cliffs, using the muscles and build of a man who'd been dead for fifty years to accomplish the disposal. As a servant, she scurried back to the queen's chambers, then readied herself for the engagement party.

She'd raise her glass that very night and toast the long and happy marriage of her daughter to the high-born Duke of Yelagin, securing their alliances in the center of the continent and freshwater resources. With her glass raised and the spineless king at her side, she'd suggest the wedding be held while the Yelagin party was there at the castle, lest they waste a week on the road, and another to return. It would be so much wiser, after all, to secure the safety of Farehold's future prince by wedding him and keeping him within his new castle. No one would disagree, and she knew it.

Moirai would be horrified, of course, but the girl had been well trained. After all, if you kick a dog enough, they don't bite back. She'd have to keep an eye on it, however, as she suspected Moirai was approaching the ideal threshold between cowering wounded creature, and violent, wrathful animal. Once she secured the marriage, she could pull back. Left to her own devices, Moirai would bear children, secure the next generation of their lineage.

Penelope would live forever, of course. Once Moirai was ready to ascend, she could take the face of an advisor, a courtier, or whatever might keep her in an influential place in the court. It would be less of a headache if Penelope could kill Moirai and take the face herself, but there was no face for her to take. She'd killed the princess as a child, and it would be the only mask she could don. The present Moirai was an illusion. Murdering her daughter would yield few results, and a multitude of inconveniences, as she'd gain nothing more than a disfigured fae of mixed, non-royal lineage in her roster of skins.

Alas, Moirai was best kept alive.

Aden supported her push to move up the wedding with sloshed toasts of sparkling wine, as did all of the wasted, slovenly partygoers. Amidst the dancing, the music, the feasting, and jovial energy of the engagement party, it was a clear that King Aden had heard nothing of the rumors of Moirai's ruined virtue. Still, Penelope had already been plotting his murder. It may as well be now. He was just drunk enough to smile when she invited him back to her rooms as the banquet drew to a close.

The act of killing itself had its blessings and curses. She enjoyed the shock on their face, sipping their surprise like a fine wine. The dopamine buzz of power was better than any drink. The blood, however, was sticky. And dead bodies were heavy. The dead weight of her freshly killed husband was no exception.

It was criminal that she was responsible for cleanup.

Fortunately, Penelope had discovered a rather delightful passage when she'd first arrived that took her directly from her chambers into the wine cellars. The only thing dusting the stairwell now was the fabric that still clung to the bodies she rolled down the steps once she disposed of them. Eventually, she'd push up her sleeves and shove them into the sea, but for now, she had no time to spare.

After all, if she wanted to see the wedding moved forward seamlessly, she had a fae male's face to don, amber liquor to spritz upon her neck, and a young heart to break.

PART FIVE
CROWN

"Cassius?" Moirai breathed the name. She'd been in the midst of ripping silver hair pins laden with pearls from her hair. The fragile latches on her corset were half torn from their placement. She'd chased away the attendants who had followed her back to her room in the wake of the banquet. She'd entered the dinner with another of an infinite line of fake smiles. She would have squeezed into the dress if she'd have ever been permitted to be fae, but in her cursed human body, it was so tight she could neither inhale nor exhale. Perhaps it was best that no one could see her true form. Without the illusion, she was no longer fit for the eye—an ancient witch clouded in wounds at the hands of her abuser. Were it not for her gift, Cassius would never have loved her. At least this way she could give him someone beautiful.

"Moirai," he responded quietly. "The engagement…"

She ran into his arms, crashing into him. He made a sharp sound as she forced the air from his lungs in his embrace. "It was horrible," she said, bodice half open, hair askew, makeup smudged. "They're pushing the wedding. Take me with you, Cass. Please. For the love of the All Mother, please."

Cassius carefully unraveled himself from her and held her at arms' length. "Everything your mother said...Moirai, I've tried for hours to wrap my head around it. How can it be true? If you're fae, why did you need me to train you in illusion? If this is truly your gift, was it not developed?"

She swallowed the tight knot into her stomach and nodded. "It was," she said. "I only knew how to hold it for myself. I don't know why my mother suspected I might be able to expand the ability. I've heard of fae having primary and secondary abilities, but this was a push to force my primary far beyond its comfortable limits. I was shocked when she brought you in, Cassius. But now you know how she knew of my power of illusion."

He nodded slowly. "You are full fae, then?"

She made a slight face. "I...no. My father was a faeling."

Cassius chewed his lip. "Show me," he said.

She blinked slowly.

"I want to see the real you." The hands that gripped her shoulders tightened slightly. His thumbs moved with slow reassurance. "Show me the face of the woman I fell in love with."

✦

Some knives are meant for bread and butter. Some serrated edges carve flesh. Others are crafted to pierce the heart. This time, the searing pain of rejection left her bleeding out from a wound she'd never fathomed.

Moirai folded herself piece after piece, becoming so small she was scarcely certain she existed after Cassius had left. She'd known she was no beauty. She hadn't seen herself without her mask for years. At first, it had been like searching for a latch deep within herself. She'd woven herself so tightly around the illusion that she scarcely knew how to unravel where the spell ended and she began. Then she kept the knots tightly fastened because of the face that looked back in the mirror. She was meant to be a perfect, ethereal fae in her second decade of life. The face that looked back when she dropped the illusion…

He'd seen her for who she was, and it was the final straw he needed to leave Aubade forever and choose Amina. She'd never forget the look of thinly veiled disgust on his face as she pulled her knees more tightly to her chest, wrapped her arms more closely around herself, and squeezed until she evaporated into a perfect, tiny nothing.

Days became a week became a wedding day.

She was a sullen bride dressed in white. Each step echoed with hallow emptiness as she passed beneath the arches, beyond the noble crowd, past the jewel tones of gowns and capes and glistening flashes of teeth that were perhaps meant to convey some semblance of joy. She was an empty husk at the end of the aisle staring listlessly into the eyes of the Duke of Yelagin. She didn't care for him, but at least he was human. No human had ever harmed her or made her feel less than. Every human could be pushed around, controlled, or manipulated. Surely, the newly crowned prince would be no exception.

Queen Penelope smiled an easy, practiced smile from her place among the courtiers and worshippers, clapping merrily at the union, and Moirai stared back with a deadpan gaze. They ate and drank and very happy things happened all around her. Queen Penelope popped in, then moved out. Moments later King Aden would drift in to greet his subjects.

Moirai knew her mouther's poisonous smile. She knew it on the king's face. She knew that the woman who'd birthed her, beaten her, and raised her had taken care of him, just as she'd sworn.

Her new husband was an average male of average height with an average dick who lasted an average time in bed. He'd had servants help her out of her wedding dress, then scarcely noticed her despondent gaze at the wall as he'd pumped into her body, push after push until he grunted in satisfied release.

He'd fallen asleep soon after, and she stared down at him with his cum dripping down her leg. With phantasmal quiet, she left the marital bed and drifted to the door that joined rooms with her mother. Drunk on wine and the joy of a scheme well-accomplished, Queen Penelope had passed out in a puff of silk sheets and ocean of pillows. A gauzy canvas hung from the four carved posts of the queen's bed, barely concealing the outline of her sleeping form.

There would be no grand proclamations. No speeches for betrayal. No confrontations.

She knew only two things: Cassius did not love her, and she would never be free from her mother's tyranny unless she took matters into her own hands.

She could not survive one thousand years of slaps, cuts, and control under a queen who refused to age. She could, however, step into the gauzy curtains and hover over her mother's sleeping form. She could lift the razor-sharp shears that rested on her vanity above her head. She could plunge them into the woman's throat, watching her eyes fly open, her blood spurt, her sheets drench with the crimson lake of her blood, her final moments of life latch onto her daughter's cold, unfeeling eyes. She could watch her mother's hands fly helplessly to the scissors, then look to her for help that would not come. She could cast the illusion of male footprints, of the red smear of a male hand, of the stumbling, bloody trail of a man who'd disappeared behind the mirrored passage her mother thought she'd so cleverly hidden. She could rid the throne of a king and queen in one fell swoop.

Perhaps she'd give her husband a year before she dealt with him. Two, if he was funny. Three months, if he was boorish. Then she'd follow the path stretched out before her. The one her father had paved, and her mother had blazed. Men disappointed, yes. Penelope had said as much.

But it was fae who'd shown her the true evils of the world. Abandonment, torture, scars, betrayal, and loss were at the hands of the pure-blooded, the magical, those who thought themselves so superior. They believed themselves gods, doing and taking and humiliating and destroying as if everyone was their plaything. At least among humans, she was safe. At least among humans, no one could hurt her.

UNTO US A PRINCESS IS BORN

ACT II

PART ONE
INHERITANCE

"The sun always shines on the tulip fields, Your Grace, even when there are clouds in the sky."

"Of course, Celeste. It's hard to frown amongst flowers." Daphne smiled sadly at her lady-in-waiting. The highborn viscount's daughter had been with her since childhood. And though they both knew the right words to say, much was left to subtext. She supposed it was a blessing to have a friend who understood you, even when nothing could be done to take the pain away.

An encouraging nod accompanied Celeste's gesture out the carriage window. "We were devastated by the hailstorms that ravaged the fields last spring! I suspect they'll be twice as beautiful this year. Absence making the heart grow fonder and all of that. I'm just sorry your mother couldn't make it."

Heaviness coated her final sentence.

"As am I," Daphne agreed, the smallest joy sparking within her. "I suppose we'll have to tour the fields and be gifted bouquets without lessons."

The warmth of the beaming smile and flash of white teeth

filled her further as Celeste said, "Bereft that we must just enjoy our time, moving at our own leisurely pace..."

"Getting mud on the hems of our gowns..."

An unadorned hand flew to Celeste's chest as she gasped. "Dirt? You jest too far. Absolute blasphemy."

Daphne giggled, and truly felt it. Celeste reached across the carriage and gave her hand a gentle squeeze. And though the gesture had been intended as comfort, it reminded her of her misery. She watched the trees grow thinner and thinner as they entered the rolling hills and rich soil of agricultural land. Her spirits settled like the dust left behind as the carriage bounced down the regency's road, silence befalling them as the women quietly ventured off to celebrate the princess's engagement.

✦

"I'm so sorry, Your Majesty," the woman fretted. Apology had drenched her words, her face, her posture from the moment she'd greeted them at the carriage and led them past the vacant fields of rich, unplanted soil, into the home. Daphne had dreamed of reds and yellows and whites, each bloom smiling up from its lush, green stock, but was met with stretches of brown. They stood in the foyer of the nearly-empty bucolic home as the lady of the house wrung her hands. "We'd sent word. We—"

Daphne reached out and touched the farmer's wife, quelling the woman's worry. The motion sent the woman into near hysterics, and Daphne didn't know how to keep the woman from crying, except to say, "Please, don't apologize. I'm happy for you and your husband. You've served Farehold well for a long time. Raascot will be lucky to have you."

Daphne had been in this home twenty times by her most modest estimates. It had never been lavish, but there were generally bouquets on the table, framed paintings on the walls, books on the shelves, and a kettle of tea whistling for anyone who wanted it. Stripped to its bones, the building was undeniably strange.

"It's just." The woman's plain face pinked. She swallowed through her emotion. "The gift of growing things has been good for years, you see? We were never a bother. But then with our boy. He's a good lad, he is. My husband and his first wife weren't blessed with children, you see. When she passed…and then the All Mother saw fit to give us a son… And I wish to the goddess that the boy had inherited his father's gift for the land. But when the people found out. And when—"

The country home vibrated. Daphne, Celeste, and the farmer's wife turned in alarm at the raucous as three bangs came from the door. Daphne heard Rigel's yell as her guard cried out in warning. The mixed noise of her coach caught her by surprise. Whatever was happening, both of her men had intervened.

"Let us in!" came an unfamiliar, masculine bark. "The crown deserves to know!"

Daphne heard the high-pitched ring of an unsheathed sword, knowing Rigel had drawn his weapon. "Stand down," came Rigel's gruff command.

"They deserve to know," the voice insisted. A moment later, the door flew open. The village men stopped short at the sight of Daphne, perhaps expecting her mother. The gruff, bovine leader removed his hat with a stiff, uncertain bow.

While the farmer's wife was in simple clothes, she was been clean, and friendly. These men wore the dirt of the field and hate on their faces.

"Your Majesty," said the leader of the ambush, words like tumbling gravel. "You have to know this family—you're standing in their very home—they've brought evil into the world, they have. We know all about the dark magics here. And if they flee to the Kingdom of Night, then northern power only grows. If you were wise—"

Daphne clasped her hands in front of her, ever the picture

of poise. She stared at the grimy silhouette that refused to step beyond the threshold, backlit by the silver gloom of the sky beyond. Unruffled, she asked, "Do you question my wisdom?"

"No, Your Highness," he said. He looked over his shoulder to see confirm the men around him were also shaking their heads. "We want safety for the world. And what sort of world—"

"What sort of world will it be," she agreed, "when the loveliest tulip farm in Farehold is banished, eliminating color and joy and beauty from our kingdom? This family has served Farehold faithfully for centuries."

"It's unnatural," the man argued.

"Mmm," Daphne agreed. "That is the glory of having the gift to grow things, isn't it? The most stunning plants in the world? Perhaps if he were as skill-free as you, he wouldn't have won the favor of the crown, earning annual visits since before either I or my mother or my mother's mother were born. We truly have benefited from this magic for a long, long time."

He stamped a foot, "But the boy! You don't know of their child, Your Highness, or you wouldn't be standing in the house of evil."

Daphne raised a testing brow as her guard approached the man from behind. Rigel clasped a hand on the man's shoulder, but the man remained unfazed. Raising her voice so the mob could hear, Daphne turned to the desperate wife and mother who still fretted before her.

Daphne's brows met in the middle. She had eyes only for the woman, heart filled with sympathy as she said, "Your child is blessed to have been born into a family who will give him his best chance at life, though Farehold will be worse-off for your absence. The All Mother has smiled upon him to gift him with parents such as you. May your journey be safe, and your lives be long and happy."

The woman seemed like she had been resisting the urge to

cry for some time, first from stress, then panic, and now it was softened, watery gratitude that lined her eyes. She used a sun-speckled hand to wipe at the tear before it fell.

The truth, Daphne knew, was that word had *not* arrived to Aubade that the tulip fields would no longer be cultivated. Given what she'd learned in the past few minutes about the villagers' opinion of the farmer's son, she had her suspicions that someone had intercepted the raven and its message intentionally. Her mother, Queen Moirai, had never been quiet about her feelings regarding magic. She wondered if prejudiced villagers had been hoping their queen might arrive to deliver a swift fist upon the farmers.

"It appears," Daphne said to the man, "that the only one giving me trouble is you. Sir, may I have your family name? So that if you'd like to register a complaint, I can tell the royal guard precisely who harangued their princess?"

He adjusted his grip on his hat. "Your Highness…"

"Or," Daphne said firmly, "you can apologize to this woman for interrupting her preparations for departure, and I can do you the magnanimous favor of forgetting this exchange occurred."

The men were too stunned to do little more than back away. Her guard shot her a look before closing the door behind the men, giving the women their privacy once more.

The royal family had been visiting the tulip fields for generations, and was under no illusions as to the farmer's mixed heritage, as he'd remained a healthy man of forty for nearly two centuries, by all accounts. Who knew how long he might have gone on to tend the kingdom's flowers had his first wife not tragically passed years before Daphne's birth. Remarrying should have been a joyous occasion, and Daphne was told it had been. His second wife was the only lady of the farm Daphne had ever known, and she believed the woman to be doing a splendid job.

Having a child should have been similarly celebrated, and

it had been. Daphne had seen the baby, then the toddler, then the bright-eyed child he'd become, enjoying watching him grow as the years went on. He'd been perfectly lovely, and the farmer's family had been similarly adored, until they weren't.

Daphne learned that, not three months prior, the farmer's son had wandered into the farmhouse with the family cat—one missing an eye and some rather important skin near its ribs—the village had seen the necromancy for what it was.

Celeste had remained quiet throughout the exchange. When she spoke from over Daphne's shoulder, it was to say, "It's customary for the royal family to be hosted in the guest cottage when they visit the tulip fields. Might we rest from the road, and return to Aubade tomorrow?"

A new emotion visibly flooded the woman. The blood drained from her face, eyes becoming as wide as teacups.

"Oh…" She swallowed audibly. "Yes, of course. Of course you may. It's just…"

Something caught Daphne's eye. She could see the cottage at the edge of the property through the window just over the woman's shoulder. She tilted her head curiously at the splash of darkness moving from the cottage doors. The black was too deep to be a shadow. The shape was too unusual to be clothes. No, it was almost as if she were looking at a bird. A bird addressing the mob of men, that was.

With a quick intake of air, Daphne understood.

"You had escorts come down from Raascot?" she whispered. Celeste's whimper at her side only exacerbated the stress crackling through her.

"No! No, Your Majesty, please—we didn't know! I didn't know he would come. The villagers were up in arms. We'd promised to leave! We weren't going to cause any trouble. He arrived of his own volition, Your Highness. He's just in the cottage while we gather our things and get on the road."

"We can leave now," Celeste whispered, voice trembling. "I'll tell the coach—"

"No." Daphne shook her head, summoning her courage. "No, I would quite like to meet these northern fae. Our kingdoms should have an open line of communication, don't you think?"

"But, Your Highness, they're barbarians." Celeste's voice hitched.

Daphne turned over her shoulder to glare. "Says Queen Moirai, who's never been anywhere or done anything. And she isn't here, is she?"

"Ma'am," Celeste implored the woman, "is it safe? For Princess Daphne?"

Cold sweat of panic that still hadn't subsided beaded over the woman's forehead. "I assure you, there is no one safer in the world. None of us would let anything happen to Her Royal Highness."

"Good," Daphne said. "Now, Celeste." She turned to face her handmaid once more. "If you and the lady of the house will find us a place to sleep for the night, I'd like to greet a fae."

Celeste shook her head vehemently. "You shouldn't go alone. Take Rigel."

"I also shouldn't get mud on my knees, but as we've established, this trip was meant for blasphemous disobedience."

"The queen will never forgive me," Celeste begged.

Daphne draped a hand over her heart. "I certainly won't be telling her. And I have reason to suspect that you won't either, right?" she asked the woman.

"Never!" the woman swore.

"Good. In that case, please see to it that you and I have a roof over our heads and a warm place to sleep before we make the return journey in the morning."

Celeste tried again. "Might the lady of the house consider relocating her Raascot...guests? The cottage is intended to house the royal family, after all."

A tear dripped from the woman's eye as she said, "That's the thing, Milady...Your Majesty... It *is* housing royalty."

✦

Daphne hadn't slept in days, save for the winks that came in the last moments before the sun rose. Purplish bruises smudged beneath her eyes, betraying her exhaustion. Celeste had made a muttering comment about how if Daphne grew any more miserable, she might resemble her mother at long last. The joke was spoken on a whisper, as the perpetual glow of her skin, the pale brown of her waves, the blush of her cheeks, the vibrant emerald of her eyes wasn't similar in the least to Moirai's severe features or her late father's rotund traits. She was a true beauty, favored by the goddess. So she'd heard on the tongues of Farehold's citizens, anyway.

She'd have to go another week without sleep before she looked half as miserable as her mother. She'd barely picked at her food. And yet...

"Shall I send for a healer?" she'd heard an attendant asked.

"No, no," Celeste had responded, shooing the woman away. "The princess is just deep in righteous contemplation. The All Mother has blessed us with a truly pious monarch." But Daphne hadn't missed the worried creases on Celeste's face as she'd shut the door, leaving Daphne alone with her thoughts for yet another day.

Laughter.

The fae had the most spectacular, honest, charming laugh she'd ever heard. She'd spent her years being prim and proper. She was cordial. She was genteel. She controlled her feelings, never wanting to upset those around her. Her mother had taught her the virtue of silence at a very young age.

Princesses didn't make a spectacle of themselves. They didn't rough house, they didn't frolic, they didn't disturb the peace.

Princesses washed their faces every day. They didn't talk back to bishops, priestesses, or their mother. They were never in a room alone with a man. And above all else, a princess was never foolish enough to go near the fae.

"Demons hide in plain sight," Moirai had said. "You may think it's someone you know, someone you trust, someone you love. The prettiest faces conceal the most terrible truths. It's why the fae are beautiful. The All Mother, in her infinite wisdom, allowed those of us with discernment to understand the balance of the world. Their faces are every bit as beautiful as their souls are ugly."

"But maybe if I could meet a fae..." Daphne had asked, scarcely eleven years of age.

"No!" Moirai had snapped. The great purge had happened when Daphne was still learning to walk and talk. Moirai had removed those with even the small magics from the castle. The rest of her life had been spent in a cautious bubble, carefully guarded from the danger of malicious power that could be lurking anywhere.

But he'd laughed.

Daphne flopped onto her back as yet another sleepless night began to fade into the gray hours of first light. She'd been so taken aback by his smile, eyes widening at how devastatingly sexy she'd found the sharpened points of his teeth. She'd tried to keep her eyes politely off his wings, but he'd extended one toward her, asking her if she'd like to touch it.

She had. The soft rainbow of blues, blacks and purples had shimmered beneath her finger. She hadn't meant to make a sound, but her appreciative exhalation had been one of true amazement.

They hadn't spoken long. Even if he weren't fae, Daphne was engaged to be married, and it wouldn't be proper to be seen chatting with a man. She'd had done her best to keep her wits about her, remembering her cautious lessons on the fae as she eyed him. She'd asked where his guard was, and he'd winked, assuring her that he was fine on his own. She'd inquired as to how he'd heard about the boy, and he'd given some intentionally cryptic answer that she'd spent days attempting to decipher. Most importantly, she wanted to know why he worried himself with the safety of one family.

"A king is a shepherd of sorts," he'd said. "Raascot is safe. They have my love, and the protection of my military. Those already securely north of the border don't need me nearly as much as the sheep who are far from the pen. This," he gestured to the farm and the village beyond— "is where the wolves are. I'm needed."

Daphne had been speechless.

She'd spent two decades being told that the fae were the predators. Hearing him describe the villagers' reaction to a boy and his family, banished for being born with something he couldn't control, she truly wondered who the villains were.

"Besides, Princess." Her heart had skipped as he looked into her eyes. "I'm particularly hard to kill. And when I care about someone or something, the rest is little but noise."

PART TWO
BIRTHRIGHT

Oh, goddess, he smelled good. She'd imagined he would, but this was sinful.

She wrapped her arms around him, slipping one hand between his wings and resting it between his shoulder blades, and the other onto the back of his neck as she tucked her face against his chest. She moaned lightly as she inhaled, losing herself to the intoxicating cloud of black currant and fresh-chopped wood and bourbon.

Her face fell, displeasure snaking into her tiny heaven as she realized he wasn't holding her in return.

"If I'm never to see you again," she muttered into his chest, "the least you can do is embrace me in my dreams."

There was that laugh. A surprised, honest sound as strong arms wrapped around her. She could feel his smile as he spoke into her hair. "You're a lucid dreamer?"

"Of course," she said dreamily. "Aren't you?"

Another laugh. He pulled away from her, inspecting her at arms' length. "That I am, Princess. But it's rare to encounter others who are."

She slipped her hand into his, enjoying the rough callouses against her soft fingers as she tugged him forward. "Well," she said, leading them over the moss-covered forest floor under the silvery light of the moon, "Iit's a blessing and a curse. Seeing things you can never have. Imagining a life that might never be. But at least here, I get to be free."

"Where is 'here'?" he asked as he followed.

She gestured as the papery birches disappeared, opening up to reveal a beautiful, marble building. "Farehold's Temple. It's one of the few places I've been permitted to go without armed guards. I enjoy the peace."

"Is peace a scarce commodity in Aubade?"

She sighed and dropped his hand. Daphne sunk to the floor, propping her back against a tree. "You're a product of my mind. You should know there is no joy in the south. Maybe that's why the goddess rewarded me with a vision of the north —if only for the night. I suppose I could make you say anything, couldn't I? Maybe that's why I dreamed of you. It would soothe me to hear that Raascot is the hellish land of nightmares I'd been led to believe. So please, King Ceres, tell me what I need to hear so that I can find reprieve."

His apology was kind as he said, "I'm afraid I can't do that."

She looked at him sharply. "This is my dream. And that's what I need. Please oblige."

"What if," he said carefully, "I told you that this dream is not yours and yours alone?"

Daphne looked out over the perfectly still night. She created a gentle breeze, creating the freshwater sound of wind as leaves rubbed together, mimicking a river. Her gaze flitted to the pond, as if remembering for the first time that there was meant to be a waterfall. She opted to keep it quiet, deciding it would be too loud for such a calm dream.

Gravity pulled her head backward, tilting her chin toward the moon as she rested fully against the thin, smooth tree. "I would say that I understand the value of pretty lies over cruel truths. Particularly if one is helpless to change their reality. And perhaps this kind deceit is one I needed to hear."

He looked at her with distinct sadness. "I have a feeling your life has not been a happy one."

"Mmm," she agreed, closing her eyes. "Is that why I've conjured you? To remind me of the unpleasantness in the world? To banish my fantasies of far-off worlds and distant escapes?"

"I came because I was curious," he said. After a long pause, he added, "And because these last few days have been miserable. I thought it would change if I got back to Raascot, but I'm still a day or more out from the border and the feeling exacerbates with every step I put between myself and the curious, clever princess who protected the farmer's family from their worst fears. You've won that family's loyalty. And, Princess, I have not stopped thinking about you."

She closed her eyes, smiling as she said, "The mind is a wicked thing."

She opened her eyes as a hand covered hers. She looked down at it, then up at its owner. She hadn't noticed how close he'd gotten. He said, "What if I could prove to you that this is more than your mind? Would you see me again?"

She ran her fingers along his jaw, then through his hair. Daphne leaned in, drinking in his scent, lips an inch from his as he breathed out when she breathed in. She tilted her chin, curious to taste the king of feathers and fae and power and dreams, but the instant before her mouth could brush against his, he turned away.

Into her hand, he muttered, "Believe me when I tell you that I would love to kiss you, Princess. And if you'll meet me, I promise to the goddess that I will. But it isn't right unless you understand how real this is."

She chuckled lightly. "How real can it be when I can start and stop the waterfall?"

He smiled at her. Goddess, his smile was unbelievable. She knew she'd spend three more sleepless nights staring at the ceiling just to live within the shimmering moment of his smile.

"You said you can come here without guards, correct? To the Temple?"

"I can."

"And," he continued, "let's say I am a product of your subconscious. If I'm your own mind, that's fine. Your mind is telling you that you're overdue for a trip to see the goddess. Either you'll arrive as a worshiper, or perhaps there will be someone there who would very much like the chance to speak with you again, if only once more. Would you concede that there's no downside to visiting the temple?"

The wind had stopped. She could hear only a heartbeat, though she wasn't sure it was hers. Was he nervous?

"And when," she asked, "would the goddess wish me to pray?"

"I can be there in five days' time," he responded. "In the morning I'll pass the family off to an outpost near the border. And then all I want is to turn around and fly south."

"Perhaps..." she mused, the sound of rustling leaves resuming as she soaked into the relaxation of the dream. "A righteous princess would do well to pray."

✦

"Your Highness, I would really feel best if you allowed me to escort you to the temple."

Daphne shook her head firmly, cool confidence at her back as she addressed her guard. "You know as well as I that men are not permitted in the temple. Tell me, Rigel, do you hear so much as a rabbit?"

Rigel's grip slackened, releasing the hilt of his sword as he examined the forest, decidedly unhappy. One guard had stayed with the coach and carriage while he walked her into the woods until the browns and grays of oaks and boxelders gave way to poplars, quaking aspen, and birch. They were close.

Still, they both knew she was right. It was the crown's fault for not employing more women in the guard if they didn't want her to go to the temple alone.

Daphne wasn't afraid of the forest.

She wasn't afraid of the temple.

She wasn't afraid of the dark, or of being alone, or of anything that went bump in the night.

The only thing she feared was the inevitable disappointment when she'd walk into the glen to find that, just as she suspected, dreams were only dreams. She'd descended into sleepless misery once more after awaking, the ghost of sweet jams and woodsy scents still clinging to her. When she'd explained to her mother and maids that what she needed was to go to the temple to pray, they'd seemed relieved.

Yes, a little religious solace might be exactly what one might prescribe the soul. Then they'd get their calm, well-behaved princess back. She'd be well-rested and pretty and agreeable once more. Perhaps it was just what the All Mother had ordered.

But as her heart pitter-pattered, as her nerves rushed through her veins, crashing in her ears louder than the waterfall, as her mouth dried and heart squeezed, the temple came into view. And along with it, a dark figure leaning casually along the building's side.

In that moment, she stepped out of the forest and back into a dream.

It was on the dreamlike cloud that she ran to him, not to greet a stranger, not to see a man she'd shared a few hours with in the countryside, or one who'd haunted her waking thoughts, or one who'd filled her sleeping hours. It wasn't even toward a devilishly handsome smile or strong arms or the thrill of disobedience as she knew she was doing something utterly forbidden.

She threw weight, her body, her entire being into the arms of the most addictive substance of all: hope.

And in that same dream, he took her from the grass into the sky. They were birds, shooting stars, floating prayers. She threw her arms back, tilting her face to the sky, letting her hair tumble through the air as it caught on the wind.

"Aren't you afraid?" he asked through a smile, holding her tightly as he soared.

She relaxed fully, trust-falling into the night. "There are far worse things than falling."

And she was right.

He wouldn't let her fall, except in love with him.

All of Aubade murmured with impressed reverence over Princess Daphne's renewed zeal. She was the kingdom's righteous flower, protecting her faith with dedicated fervor as she made weekly treks to the temple to worship at the foot of the All Mother. She'd spend all night in passionate devotion, returning to the carriage the next morning with clear eyes, a buoyant heart, and with the glow of someone deeply in love—with the goddess, that was.

Spring became summer became the first distant warning of fall.

She'd been wading through the creek, picking smooth, shiny rocks in the moonlight with her dress bundled as a make-shift apron while Ceres watched from the riverbank.

"Come in with me!" she called.

"And get eaten by river monsters?" he chuckled. "You be the fish, and I'll be the bird."

"I'll be the mermaid," she called back, "and you'll be the angel." The water bit at her ankles, chilling her more quickly than normal. She returned with her collection and handed them gleefully to Ceres. "For the royal treasury."

She squealed as he pulled her against him. "I can think of something that Gwydir needs more than smooth rocks. Though they are very pretty."

"They are, aren't they?" She continued turning them over in her hand. It took her a while to realize he hadn't looked away. "What?"

"Come to Gwydir with me."

He smile faded slowly. She set down her rock and looked out over the river. "I'm to be wed this winter." She tossed one of her precious pieces into the water. "To a man I've met exactly twice." She threw another stone, this one quite a bit harder. "Who's twenty years my elder"—another loud splash —"and whose only redeeming quality is that he holds the land that borders Tarkhany. It's the advantageous marriage of the century," she grunted, arm cranked for her final toss when he caught her hand.

"Say," he chastised softly, "these belong to Raascot's Royal Treasury. I'm quite fond of them."

She looked away.

He ran his fingers through her hair, cupping her head gently as he said, "What if I were to propose a marriage far more advantageous than a lord with some land to the south."

She looked up at him with eyes that scarcely dared to hope.

"Marry me, Daphne."

She felt the tears drip onto the bare skin just above her bodice before she even realized she was crying. She wrapped her ringers around his hand, holding it more tightly to her.

"My mother would sooner go to war…" She left the second part unsaid, though they both heard it. *Than wed me to a fae.*

"Your mother is terrible," he agreed. "But I want to take that gamble. I think her thirst for power may just be enough. Is her hate greater than her greed?"

And this gave Daphne pause, for she did not know the

answer. An entire kingdom was a tempting offer, with ten thousand ways to spin the proposal. Maybe Moirai would see it as an opportunity for control, as a way to influence, as a way to turn the tide in Farehold's favor. She didn't care how her mother saw it. But perhaps all hope was not lost.

"I should soften her first," Daphne said cautiously.

"No, no." Ceres kissed her knuckles. "It should never be your responsibility to take the brunt. Let me shelter you. I'll arrive with a formal proposal, as a king. I'll come with thirty royal dowries in gifts and bring only my most talented, benevolent, and inoffensive subjects. Perhaps she hates us only because she's never been exposed to us. Most hate is born of ignorance."

Daphne chewed on his words. She nodded slowly. "Ceres, I want nothing more. I want to spend all my days with you, even if the Kingdom of Night really is a place of nightmares and evil and—"

He splashed her with his foot. She swatted at him as he said, "You think I'd bring you to the north if it was *anything* like the campfire stories you've been told? Come with me! Let me show you."

Daphne frowned at the position of the moon. "We have a few more hours at best, Ceres. I have to be back, unless you're willing to abduct me and meet Farehold in open war. But you know I'd never forgive myself if a single one of your people died over my selfishness."

He pressed a kiss into her hair. "And you say that even while believing it's the kingdom of nightmares. Sleep with me."

She looked at him with wry judgement. "Again? You're insatiable."

He grinned. "I am. But, truly, fall asleep with me. Let me take you to Gwydir. Let me walk you through the castle and show you the kingdom. Generally, when we sleep—walk together we're…"

"Distracted."

"Distracted," he agreed, fingers tightening against her hip. Her blood heated as she said a silent prayer of thanks to the goddess for their sensual, incredible, volcanic dreams.

"Do your men miss you?" she asked.

He pulled back, eyes twinkling with amusement. "I know you've heard a thing or two about the debaucherous fae, but are you thinking of groups of men when I'm inside you?"

She squealed, punching him in the arm. "You're terrible! You said you used your gift to visit your outposts and military and people before you met me. You see me nearly every night. Is Raascot okay? Am I…"

"Are you destroying my kingdom because I can't pull myself away from you? Well, you are quite powerful." He kissed her deeply, and she lost herself in the swirl of heat and safety before he rested her forehead against hers. "No. My troops are perfectly competent—and unlike Farehold, anyone can serve. Aside from a skirmish along the mountains, every-thing's perfectly quiet."

"A skirmish?" she repeated, looking up at him with concern.

"My cousin serves as general. It's a well-earned title. I would be a poor king if I didn't trust him, and I do. He's level-headed, wise, and when he makes a call, I believe him. He has it handled."

"Your cousin…" She said the words slowly, wondering why she hadn't spent more time asking about his kingdom, his family, his life. They'd been rather busy. Finally, she said, "Yes, I'd like to see Gwydir. I'd love to see your world. Your throne. Your trees and sunsets and even what you eat for dinner. Though, truth be told, I think I might be too excited to sleep."

Ceres flipped her onto her back, cradling her head before it hit the stones. His mouth was on her throat a moment later as he rumbled, "Come with me, my queen. I bet I can help you sleep."

PART THREE
REIGN

"Mother, stop."

Queen Moirai threw the fabric to the ground, reminding Daphne more of a toddler throwing a tantrum than a woman in a discussion. Such had been her life. Daphne had grown accustomed to managing her mother's emotions. The kingdom depended on it.

"I have not pushed," Moirai said icily, "but you have put this off for far too long. You are mere weeks away from your wedding, Daphne. I ask so little." They stood amidst silk and chiffon and lace and all of the things a bride was supposed to enjoy in the weeks leading up to her wedding. Her mother had told her many times that she hadn't cared much for~~her~~ the late king, but that even if political marriages were only for name, a wedding could still be beautiful. As irritable as she was, Daphne truly saw a strained, undercurrent of kindness to her mother's words. She wanted the wedding to be special, in whatever small way it could be.

Daphne raked her fingers through her hair. She kept her

eyes closed as she said, "I've spent a lot of time in prayer as of late. And the goddess continues to give me a message."

Moirai looked down at the discarded fabric. "Does the All Mother have a preference regarding tulle and embroidery?"

"No," Daphne said patiently. "I feel I'm being told to wait, should another suitor—a better suitor—present themselves."

Moirai's laugh came out in a single bark. "Is this the resistance? Child, this is the best match in all of Farehold—and that's including the consideration of marrying you to the count who owns the land on which the university rests."

"The count is twelve!" Daphne gasped, eyes wide.

Moirai waved a hand. "Yes, it's not ideal. His title is inferior and his lands are lesser. Perhaps you don't like him, but believe me, Daphne, that's okay. I didn't like my husband."

"Mother..." Daphne frowned, not wishing to hear of her father in such a way.

"Royalty rarely have the chance to like their betrothed, Daphne," Moirai said, touching her daughter's elbow gently. "But you'll remain in the castle. You'll remain in power. He'll be a means to an ends. A secured allegiance. Important lands."

"How important are the lands?" Daphne groaned. "Nothing grows that far south! He's the Duke of the Desert! No one has heard from Tarkhany in a million lifetimes."

"Your propensity for hyperbole is absurd, Daphne. Truly, what kind of queen will you make?"

"One of the deserts, apparently," she grumbled, kicking the fabric.

"Daphne!" came Moirai's sharp intake of air, eyes wide. "I'm surprised at you. What has gotten into you? I did not raise you to act out like this."

Daphne strained against the urge to scream.

"Truly!" Moirai pressed. "Tell me, what about your life has been so terrible? Were you not fed? Were you not clothed? Were you ever mistreated? Were you—"

"Kept in a prison, mother!" she cried, giving in to her urge.

"A prisoner who has nightmares of being dragged by her hair down the aisle. I've done everything you've asked of me my entire life. I've been good. I've never let you down. And my reward is a life of punishment. Please, don't be cruel."

"Cruel!" The queen's face went red.

Daphne took an uncertain step back.

"What do you know of cruelty?" she snapped, a vein throbbing on her forehead. "You haven't gotten everything you've wanted and you paint it as persecution? Your dress is green instead of yellow so you cry?" Her lips pulled back, words ringing off the walls as she howled, "You don't find your royal, advantageous, indispensable marriage favorable so you scream martyr? I have failed the kingdom if I've raised a spoiled ingrate."

Daphne rose to the occasion, matching her mother scream for scream. "It is not wrong to wish something more for my life than to be a silent hostage to another's agenda!"

The slap rang out high and loud. Daphne's hands flew to her cheek, holding the welt as heat spread through the wound. Moirai stood before her, rage trembling off her like water droplets from a wet dog for a long time. Daphne still hadn't looked at her mother when the queen turned and abandoned the room, leaving her utterly alone.

✦

"Ceres." Daphne wrapped his hands around his arm, gripping him helplessly. The iridescent shimmer of his wings disappeared against the oil-slick stones, colors so magical they belonged only in a raven's shimmer or the coldest, sparkling depths of night. She loved when their dreams took place in Gwydir. His memories were full of kindness, of freedom, of smiling faces. Anger and fights and pain rarely found them here. She hated bringing discord to their perfect hiding place. "Please, Ceres, it's fine. I'm fine."

"She struck you," he snarled, tearing his eyes from the welt. "You are not fine."

"Listen to me," she begged. "I shouldn't have come. I should have waited until the mark went away. I didn't think it would appear in the dream. It wasn't right of me to worry you."

From his look, she expected him to be angry. But he swept her up in his arms, crushing her to him as he said, "You were hurt, and you're apologizing? Daphne, I have to get you out of there. Your wedding is weeks away. We need to let all of Farehold know the wedding is off well before your boar of a fiancé departs his lands. No preparations will be wasted. No time will be lost. We'll leave from Raascot today. I wanted to bring my least-obvious fae, but time has forced our hand. We'll fly, and be there by week's end."

Emotion crashed over her, and she knew why.

Love alone hadn't pushed her to the edge with her mother.

Angst over a tempestuous wedding wouldn't have started that fight.

She and Ceres had a plan. They'd wanted to win Moirai with honey rather than vinegar. She'd pushed him off and they'd waited. He'd respected her wish time and time again as the season changed. But something else pumped through her blood. Something new, overwhelming, and terrifying.

"We're out of time," she whispered, listening to the strong heart that thundered only for her.

"I know," he said, breath hot against her hair as he covered her with reassuring kisses. "I will be there in a moment. I won't take no for an answer. You wanted me to wait, and it killed me, but I waited. I can't leave you there a moment longer, Daphne. I know you don't want a war, but I'd sooner raze the earth than leave the one I love in Aubade."

"Ceres…" Her throat constricted. Her head spun.

The dream rippled around them.

"It isn't just me any longer. I'm pregnant."

PART FOUR
DYNASTY

No bells had rung. There was no town crier, no pomp, no royal celebration for the child brought into the world.

She'd insisted on giving birth amidst women of the cloth, and given her reputation for piety, no one in the kingdom batted a lash. For her final month of pregnancy, she retreated to spend her final days in religious contemplation, as was her right. She would give birth amidst the holy women so her child might be anointed by the All Mother with its first breath.

Her husband had grunted something about sending a raven if it was a boy, and with that, she'd left.

It was not her last month of pregnancy, however.

Daphne was days away from childbirth when she arrived at the convent of matrons, rather than the summer solstice birth that had been forecasted. Even in her groans of labor, she'd screamed for the midwife to swear upon her soul to the All Mother that anything that happened on the labor bed would be for the goddess to judge—and the goddess alone. Celeste had been the only other soul permitted in the room for the birth, apart from the matron. The handmaid stared at the matron as she waited for the woman's promise.

The midwife hadn't required the threat. Daphne saw the compassion in her eyes, and trusted her with her life as the woman guided her through the labor. The screams, the sweat, the blood, the hot towels, the pain...it couldn't be for nothing.

"It's too soon," the matron had said, face creased with worry as Daphne swung her feet over the edge of the bed in the minutes after passing the afterbirth. The matron had scarcely had time to clean the baby and return it to Daphne's breast before the princess was on her feet. "Please, rest. The All Mother will protect you. I will—"

Daphne grabbed the matron's hand. "Please, hold this goodness, and do not let the world harden you," she begged. "I have to go now. It's a night with no moon, and these secrets..."

The matron's plea, her sorrow, her pain was plain on her face.

"It has to be now," Celeste urged. "Surely, others have heard her cries of labor. No one else can know."

The matron nodded, knowing the women were right.

"I can postpone any visits to your room. As far as the convent knows, you're under strict bedrest after a false labor. We won't let anyone know a babe came early," the matron said. "Return here when you've done what you need to do."

Daphne closed her eyes, sweat dripping down her face. "This secret will die with us. And the continent will be safer for it. We're doing the right thing."

"And if we're not," the matron said, "it will be the All Mother's responsibility. Come with me, Princess."

She guided Daphne to the building's edge, matron on one arm, Celeste on the other. The expression on Rigel's face told her that he'd heard every scream, every pant, every moment of labor. He was ready.

And he did not fail her.

Two women and a royal guard hurried to a carriage. But they were not alone.

"Stop!" The watchman extended a gloved hand, standing between the desperate party and their escape. Daphne's eyes widened in panic. She looked from her friend to her guard, too scared to cry as she clutched her precious bundle.

"Don't make me do this," Rigel said through gritted teeth, winter winds blowing between them.

"Sir, I can't let you—"

He wasn't given the chance to finish his thought. Rigel cut the man down where he stood. Pain creased his face just as blood coated his sword as he gestured the women forward. "Go, go!" He shoved Celeste into the carriage, watching as she held her hands out for the tightly swaddled bundle. He helped Daphne in, throwing a look over his shoulder as hounds sounded their warning. She exhaled as the door closed, but refused to let herself cry.

She received the rest she was due. Though the bed of carriage was not an ideal resting cot, she slept. And woke. And slept. When she woke again, the babe was hungry. A daughter, born with a full head of night-dark hair, just like her father. She nursed her, hoping the heat and salt of her tears wouldn't upset her perfect, beautiful infant as she wept.

"We could run," Celeste said, choking through the words. "I'll keep you both safe and warm. I'd run with you anywhere. We could hide. I'd find a way to shelter you both, whatever it took. We could—"

"No." Daphne's tears flowed freely. "We'd hide to no end. My mother would never stop looking. My husband…" She refused to waste these precious moments on him, a man so lost to whiskey and anger that her bruises and split lips could scarcely be concealed with the healing tonics stored in the castle, and that was while he believed her to be carrying his child. The man had armies and forces and lands. It was why Moirai had found the marriage so advantageous at the start.

"And...the father?" Celeste asked, harsh winter winds howling against the carriage, swallowing the final words of her question.

Daphne closed her eyes, looking only at her miracle as it suckled contentedly at her breast, feeling only the warmth and intensity of its mother's fierce affection as she held it. "This child is born of love, Celeste," she said, struggling to keep her composure. "Her father loved me more than any man has ever loved a woman, and I him...and I refuse to sully his name by speaking it on Farehold soil."

Of course, Daphne knew why she couldn't escape north.

She'd been there when her mother had exploded as an agent of hell, a conduit for demonic intent as she'd turned Ceres into a monster without the gift for speech when he'd arrived in Aubade to ask for her hand. His beautiful wings had become sinewy, his gorgeous eyes the glossy black of draconian lore. Where his hands had held her, talons remained. While he made no move to harm her, and though he seemed to possess the intelligence of a man, he was a man no longer.

She would spend her days searching for a cure, if it took months, if it took years, if it took a lifetime.

But Daphne didn't have a lifetime.

Days bled into a week before their carriage changed its tune, the snow-packed dirt road tumbling over the cobblestones of a courtyard. She'd heard little of the northern towns, but had memorized the religious institutions over the months that stretched between Ceres's transformation and her labor. This had to be it.

Daphne wasn't ready.

She looked up at Celeste with panic in her eyes. Again, Celeste said, "We could run."

And it plunged into her heart, carving it out and leaving it on the carriage floor. She knew it would never reenter her body. There was nowhere to run. There was nowhere to go. Her daughter would never be safe. Not with her blond bastard of a husband and the hate in his heart. Not with her spiteful mother and her bitterness toward the north. Daphne had made one perfect thing in her life, and it was this. No one could ruin this.

Despite their time on the road, Rigel stopped her when the carriage opened, sorrow carving lines into his face. "Your Highness, is there any other solution?"

She looked at him through the blur of tears as she shook her head, holding her head high as he stepped aside. He and Celeste flanked her as she led the way, though it was his gloved hand that pounded on the door.

It took an eternity for the door to open, and yet, it was no time at all. She could have stood there for a year, and it wouldn't have been enough time.

A middle-aged woman in gray linens opened the door, glaring up at them against the cold winds and late hour. Daphne watched the cogs turn in the woman's mind as recognition became shock. She ushered them onto the landing, closing the door against the cold and lighting the nearby torch as she muttered incomprehensible something-or-others.

"What's your name?" Daphne asked the woman at long last.

She sputtered against the question, eyes wide and white. "Agnes," she choked. "I'm the Gray Matron here. My name is Agnes."

"Agnes," Daphne said, tears spilling freely over her face, "I need you to swear something on the All Mother."

The Gray Matron nodded, too shocked to do little more. Daphne heard the stir of others in the manor, but kept her eyes fixed on this woman alone.

"By the love and wrath and blessings and curses of the All Mother, I need you to protect my daughter. Set her aside. Keep her safe. Don't let anyone touch her. Keep her close. Keep her…"

Daphne's voice broke. The babe fussed, and she pulled her

daughter close, clutching her to her breast as her tears became audible. Celeste wrapped her arms around her, holding both her and the child. Rigel stood to the side, his empathy tangible enough to be a separate party in the room as he watched her shatter.

"Agnes," Daphne said again, fighting for strength. "Her name is Nox. You are not to change it. No matter what. She needs to know. She needs to be connected. She needs…" Daphne began to tremble.

Agnes stretched out her hands to receive the babe, tenderness filling her expression, softening her posture, changing the energy of the room itself.

"She's a princess," Daphne insisted. She looked at Celeste, and her handmaid nodded, procuring a circular piece of jewelry. "Safeguard the secret. Don't do it for me, or for her. Don't even do it for the kingdom. Do it because it's right."

Agnes attempted to receive the bundle, peering down at it with wide eyes, but Daphne would not release her daughter.

"There's one more thing," came Rigel's voice behind her. "We're in need of a babe. A boy is ideal, but any would do. Yellow of hair. Anything that could pass as a newborn."

Agnes looked up at them, face flashing. "I don't have any newborns. I have one who's maybe six months—"

"He won't know the difference," Celeste insisted at her side. "Bring us the six-month-old. We have to leave with him now."

The woman nodded numbly. The Gray Matron disappeared up the stairs, leaving Daphne on the landing with her daughter for their final stolen moments.

Daphne fell to her knees, holding her daughter to her as she sobbed, "Nox, you deserve so much more than you can be given. You deserve love, and safety, and kindness. You should never be afraid. You should know how powerful you are. You shouldn't live in fear of terrible men, but be so overcome with your worth that they fall at your feet. I may not be beside you, but I will cover you with my love every step of your way. I'm doing the best I can with what I have, and I won't stop until I've fixed this. You deserve the world."

AFTERWORD

Remain in Gyrradin with completed *The Night and Its Moon* quartet and accompanying novellas. The villain duology, *A Chill in the Flame*, and *A Frozen Pyre* reveal the creation of the continent's demons, the origin of Uaimh Reev and the league of peacekeeping assassins, and the last fae royals of Farehold.

CONTENT WARNINGS

trigger warning for on-page instances of childhood abuse from a parent (mother-daughter), themes of revenge, language, sexuality, alcohol, xenophobia and attempts to overcome or confront ethnocentrism, violence, murder

THE DEER AND THE DRAGON

NO OTHER GODS

Read on for an excerpt of the urban mythology series

CHAPTER ONE

April 15, age 26

I stared down the barrel of the lesser of two evils: the flesh-and-blood disappointment of a human man, or a life trapped in my imagination with a fictional lover.

I remembered reading that the brain stops forming at twenty-six. I watched the man across from me chew his food with his mouth slightly ajar, not bothering to swallow before he went on to name-drop yet another notch in society's belt. He was holding his chopsticks wrong. He had mixed wasabi directly into his soy sauce. He'd spoken at a cringe-worthy volume throughout the meal, drawing curious, if disgruntled, stares. There wasn't a single etiquette he followed, and it wasn't even close to the worst thing about him.

I wasn't sure if I hoped the bit about the brain was true. I was halfway through my twenty-sixth year and not so sure that this was the finished product I wanted for my mind. I was doing my best to be normal. This was what normal people did, right? They went on terrible dates with ordinary humans. They didn't see things that weren't there. They didn't cling to ghosts and maladaptive fantasies they'd conjured in the dark. They took their meditations, they went to therapy, and they learned how to distinguish what was real.

If my brain had stopped forming, however, it might come with perks. On the one hand, it meant that this bovine-mannered date wouldn't be a core memory. The man in the suit across from me—Jared? Joshua? I'm pretty sure it was Josh—would be a forgettable date after a long string of mediocre sex and dating apps. On the other hand, maybe it meant my courtship habits and hidden, wish-fulfilling coping mechanisms were cemented in stone and there was no hope for me. Perhaps I was doomed to repeat a cycle of Joshes. This was my curse.

"Marlow?"

Oh, fuck. He was staring at me. Had he asked me a question? I squinted my eyes slightly, peering through the din of the too-expensive restaurant and the polite chatter of upscale patrons for a clue.

"Come again?" I attempted an apologetic smile.

His perplexed look was one I understood. Of course he would be confused that I hadn't been listening. This was our second date, and he expected more from me. After all, I'd been utterly delightful last time. Painted, waxed, and squeezed into the most stunning dress, sporting the glossiest hair and the most charming smiles, I was a living superlative. I'd spent my life learning how to make the perfect first impression.

My profile had been curated to snag any curious suitor. First was a high-resolution picture that a friend had taken four years prior on a boat in Rio de Janeiro, where the greens and grays of the coast matched my eyes. "Where was that picture taken?" gave prospective dates an easy conversation opener. The next two had been selected to attract the outdoorsy types, from the HD pic of me flexing on a mountain in yoga pants and a sports bra to me on the beach laughing with friends—which also created the perfect excuse to show off a bikini body and gave me an easy way to screen out anyone who didn't like curves. I rounded out the profile with a picture of me alone with my coffee cup and computer, looking very serious and business-like, immediately followed by a photo of me jumping on the bed holding a bottle of wine, dress flying up, muddy blond curls a cloud around my face, smiling as if I were having the time of my life. Whatever dream you wanted to project onto me, I gave you the option right there in my intricately tailored series of images.

"Who are you?" the app had asked.

"Whoever you need me to be," my profile replied.

Every date was spent in a song and dance of asking the right questions, laughing at the right pitch, tossing my hair over my shoulder, arching my neck, lowering my lashes, and, as always, keeping them talking. They'd leave thinking they'd met their soulmate. I'd leave wondering if I could catch the newest episode of *Fire and Swords* or if I'd have to wait until it was on a streaming service.

"I asked if you've been to the Galápagos," he repeated.

"No." I kept my tone as light as possible. I glanced down at the elaborately plated omakase sushi that had doubtlessly cost more than half of the country made in a month. This was why I'd agreed to go on the second date. I loved good sushi, and free just so happened to be my favorite price. The salmon belly was the most well marbled in the hemisphere. I'd come back with terrible company just to eat my weight in the stuff even if it meant thinking about what sort of life these ocean animals had before they ended up on my plate.

He grabbed the sake kettle and tilted the alcohol into his glass first, then mine.

I kept the disarming smile on my face as I said, "I've wandered my way through a lot of South America, but I was teaching English as a second language and I—"

"Oh, you have to go back and do it the right way. I have a friend who works at the most incredible resort you've ever seen. The fish swim right underneath..." His mouth kept moving as my thoughts drifted into the restaurant's ambience while I started to think of marine life. I liked aquariums. I wondered how long it had been since I'd been to one. Maybe I'd go to the city's aquatic zoo, bring a bag of magic mushrooms, pop in my headphones, and listen to music while counting sharks over the weekend.

Josh required little encouragement to continue the conversation. It only took a pleading look to the waitress and a firm "*No,*" when asked if we wanted desserts for her to bring the check without waiting for his argument on digestifs. She knew from the very intentional way I'd selected designer pieces, from the delicate chain around my neck to the bag that dangled over the back of my chair, that I could afford the bill if I'd requested it. My deadpan stare challenged him to give it to me. In my early twenties, I would have rushed to cover the check so that Josh wouldn't expect anything from me. Now I expected him to procure his Amex as penance for making me watch him chew with his mouth open. It was the least he could do.

I idly wondered if Josh had ever asked me what I did for a living. Perhaps that was my own fault. I'd gotten so good at getting others to talk about themselves that I'd become excellent at living in the shadows. I wonder how many of my dates knew more about me than my name and how spectacular I was in bed.

We'd scarcely stepped into the cold, cloudless night before he asked, "So, should we go back to my place?"

"Oh." I pouted slightly to underscore my feigned regrets while shrugging into my coat, saying, "I'm so sorry. I called a rideshare while I was in the bathroom. It's only two minutes out."

Josh looked like he'd been slapped. I wondered how many times a man with a forty-thousand-dollar Rolex was turned down. Then again, it had been a running pleasure of mine to play catch and release. The bigger the fish, the more satisfying it was to throw them back into the water. Everything about this evening had me wishing I'd stayed in to watch the documentary about whales rather than wasting the perfume by stepping out into the world.

"What about the concert?"

I frowned, scarcely looking up from my phone. "Concert?"

Confusion faded into agitation as he studied my face. "Next week, the one I—"

Fish. Everything about this man was a fish. When they tell you that there are plenty of fish in the sea, they forget to mention that half of marine life is boring, scaly and a part of an identical school of thousands just like him. I would rather be alone, high, and looking at tropical fish next weekend. "Oh, I'm so sorry, Josh—this is my car!"

"It's Jacob."

I grimaced. I really was sorry about that one. I should have checked his name from the dating profile when I'd escaped to the restroom.

He knew the evening had soured but still had the balls to go in for a kiss. I intercepted with a side hug before launching into the street to stop my car. I closed the door and took off into the night before my date had time to recover from his wounded ego. The driver asked precisely the right number of questions, which was zero. He left me alone to the buzzing phone that illuminated the back seat of the vehicle.

(Kirby) How was the banker?
(Nia) CFO, right? Big money
(Kirby) Not like tech guy. Mar, could you call him up again?
We used to go to much nicer places when you were
sleazing it with the tech guy.
(Marlow) I'd like to sleaze it up with a loose bag of cheese
and my sweatpants
(Nia) You were supposed to get laid. How am I supposed

to live vicariously through you if you're pulling a celibacy
act
(Kirby) No, that's fair. She's always been a slut for cheese.
No one made you get married, Nia.
(Nia) And so what? I'm supposed to live with the conse-
quences of my actions?
(Marlow) I'm just going to call it an early night
(Nia) And waste a great hair and makeup day? Damn, there
must be some fantastic cheese back at your place

I clicked the button on the side of my phone, turning the screen into an obsidian mirror and leaned my head against the window, watching the black and auburn blur of homes, shadows, lawns, and fences as we crossed through a neighborhood. I used to look at houses and wonder about the lives of the people who lived inside. What did the family do to afford a home so close to downtown? What did a three-story house with fantastic landscaping cost in one of the world's flashiest cities? It had been a long time since I'd cared.

I saw the driver frown as the GPS turned into the northern part of the metropolis. It wasn't an unusual reaction. No one lived in the warehouse district. There was no reason for a girl of any repute to take a car to the warehouses in high heels and red lipstick. He pulled up along the sidewalk and eyed what had once been a bread factory. His expression deepened into worry at the smattering of lights and darkened entryway.

"Is this right, miss?"

"Home sweet home." I smiled. I flashed him my screen to show the glowing rating I'd sent his way as I slid out of the car. His eyebrows remained knit, but he shrugged as I closed the door. He wasn't paid enough to care.

A blanket-like quiet pressed in as the car pulled away—a sound challenging to achieve anywhere in the city. There was no traffic, no pedestrians, no indication that anyone but the phantoms of long-dead industry tycoons haunted these corridors. The April night clung to the last of spring's chill, sending goose bumps up and down my bare legs. I fished a metallic rose-gold card from my purse and pressed it against the panel, satisfied when it buzzed.

I rounded the brick corridor for the atrium, where an ever-attentive receptionist waited to respectfully greet me. She was one of four and arguably my favorite. No matter how short my skirt, how high my heels, or how late the hour, she remained polite without speaking. I knew her boyfriend's name, I gave her chocolates every holiday, and we never failed to gush about the new episodes of *Fires and Swords* if I loitered in the hallway, but she had an innate gift for knowing when I was overwhelmed and needed silence. Perhaps intuition was a prerequisite for anyone who took a job in luxury apartments.

Though she'd never say it outright, her expressions conveyed the same long-standing concern that I'd stumbled through the door after too many dates to count. She'd helped me get into the building when I was a bit too drunk to see my phone and buzzed me up to my room whenever I'd lost too much brain function to recall how my card worked. It seemed like a safe bet that she was not the sort of person who got high at aquariums.

The small bank of polished elevators waited quietly, all in disuse given the lateness of the hour. One opened for me the moment I pressed the button.

I didn't wait for the elevator doors to close before slipping out of my heels, dangling the sharpened ends from one hand. I caught the brief, disapproving narrowing of eyes through the rapidly closing doors and flashed my most dazzling smile. Part of me respected her bravery. It was bold to be judgmental of the residents when they knew precisely how much these apart-ments cost.

I pressed the glittery, metallic card onto the pad to gain access to my floor—second from the top. The penthouse hadn't been available, and I'd been okay with it. Everyone who lived here had their reasons for wanting to stay off the world's radar, and there wasn't a better establishment in the city for those with deep enough pockets to erase themselves from the map. The building's discretion had been worth the downgrade, and as someone who lived alone, I couldn't have justified the extra space unless I was looking to install a private bowling alley.

The elevator door opened noiselessly onto my floor. There were thirteen units in the entire building—two per floor, save for the lucky bastard who'd snagged the thirteenth. I walked barefoot down the sparkling black marble to my room and pressed my thumb into the pad, allowing it to scan my fingerprint until a subtle click told me the mechanisms had unlocked.

It was dark in my apartment and stayed that way. I'd had the features for automatic lights disabled the day I'd moved in.

I tossed my purse onto the floor, leaving it in a jumble with my shoes. I walked to the window and stared out over the twinkling lights of the city and the sliver of river I could spot from my unit. I was a sucker for a good view.

The hairs on the back of my neck prickled in the way they did when one knew they were being watched. The rush of gin, moss, and mist filled the room the moment before I heard it. I breathed it in like a prayer.

"Leave it open" came a male voice from the shadows.

I fought the deep, conflicting bloom that emanated from somewhere near my center. My toes curled, heart thundering at the purr of his voice. "Don't do this to me," I grumbled half-heartedly, but I was certain he heard the ghost of a smile in my voice.

"Didn't go well?" he asked.

I continued facing the window but reached over my head for the zipper. Years had gone by, and I was still breathless every time he spoke. It was so easy to lose my resolve whenever those silken words tumbled over his lips. I managed to give the thin metal a tug but lost my grip on it as I said, "He was utterly forgettable."

"They all will be," he said, brushing my hair away from my neck. Goose bumps started at the nape of my neck and slithered down my spine. He held the top of my dress in one strong hand, using the other to gently tug the zipper. He stopped before releasing it more than a quarter of an inch. I waited for the next sensation, but nothing came. Tension swelled as I swallowed another deep breath of earth and perfume.

"What?" I breathed.

The electric current of his touch coursed through me.

"Holy fuck," I murmured, falling to pieces.

His fingers began to work their way up the hem of my dress, nudging it up over my hips. My stomach clenched. My lips parted in a stifled gasp, eyes closing as he came up behind me. His mouth sucked gently on the tender place where my throat met my shoulder. Every sense in my body homed in on the delicious sensation. His mouth moved to the back of my neck, hands dropping from my hips to urge me forward. I leaned into the floor-to-ceiling glass, letting the cold seep into me as his hand slid from my inner thigh, higher, *higher*.

"Oh god," I gasped when he grazed the soaked evidence of my black-lace panties.

"You know better than that," he chided softly at my choice in words, a teasing warmth in his voice. He relaxed his body into mine until I was pressed wholly against the window. "Now, are you going to let me in?"

My face betrayed the battle going on in my head and heart. My body ached for him. My breasts peaked against the thin dress. The pulsing in my chest extended into every piece of me, and I felt my heartbeat in my greediest places. My fingers clenched against the glass. He chuckled lightly.

"Nothing without your permission," he said, fingers still grazing me with tantalizing slowness. The tingle of the water between my legs trickling onto my inner thighs elicited a low groan of approval. His fingers continued to move over the thin fabric.

I gasped against the sensation, and he leaned into my throat once more, smiling through my pleasure.

"You know I'm…" Words felt useless.

"You're what?" he pressed me into the window with more force.

"I'm trying to stop."

His fingers quickened as he said, "As if I don't know you, Love. We both know it'll never make you happy. But if you'd prefer mundane restaurants and forgettable men over what I can offer you…" His hand stilled.

My lust, my greed, my denial came out in a single, short sound. My eyes opened as I turned back to the shadows, but I knew what I'd see before I turned.

Despite the bandage-tight dress around my hips and the puddle of evidence on my legs, I knew he wasn't there. He hadn't been there in a long, long time.

THE DEER AND THE DRAGON
NO OTHER GODS

This new series from Piper CJ is the start of an urban fantasy based on the real world. As war looms, it's a fight for survival, a pantheon of deities and a belief in love, all working together to build an epic narrative.

"HOW DOES A HUMAN GIRL LOSE THE PRINCE OF HELL?"

Marlow needs to believe she's crazy. The alternative would mean embracing the gift—or curse—shared by her mother and grandmother: she can see angels and demons, including a dark and haunting entity who's been with Marlow her entire life. At least, she believes that's all he is until a fae from the Nordic pantheon strolls into her life and informs her that she's been sharing a bed with the Prince of Hell.

A Prince who's now gone *missing*.

Before she knows it, Marlow is deeply entangled in a centuries-old war, stumbling straight into a battleground between mighty beings of myth and legend from powerful pantheons around the world. And who will come out on top may just depend on her and the love she never dared to believe in.

FOR FANS OF:
- Romantasy
- Mythology & folklore
- Kickbutt heroines
- Fae, angels, and demons
- Hilarious banter
- *Hazbin Hotel*

ABOUT THE AUTHOR

Piper CJ, author of the USA Today bisexual fantasy series *The Night and Its Moon*, urban mythology series *No Other Gods*, and New York Times bestselling series *Fern's School for Wayward Fae*, is a photographer, hobby linguist, and French fry enthusiast. She has an M.A. in Folklore and a B.A. in Broadcasting, which she used in her former life as a morning-show weather girl, hockey podcaster, and in audio documentary work. Now when she isn't playing with her dog, she's gaming, binging cartoons, dissecting fairy tales, or disappointing her parents.

website: pipercj.com

instagram.com/piper_cj
tiktok.com/pipercj

www.ingramcontent.com/pod-product-compliance
Lightning Source LLC
Chambersburg PA
CBHW071132100726

47908CB00008B/2579